THE COTTON BOLL QUEEN

J LemeThompson

Crafted with patience and purpose

Dedication

To anyone whose work has been called invisible, whose worth has been measured by shame instead of skill, and who has turned necessity into quiet power anyway.

I took my Power in my Hand—
And went against the World—
'Twas not so much as David—had—
But I—was twice as bold—
— Emily Dickinson

Chapter 1

In August, when the cotton outside Yazoo City, Mississippi began to split open like quiet explosions across the fields, Annabelle Lee Crump worked the night shift at Phil's Fill-R-Ups.

The bolls were nearly ready for harvest. The air was wet enough to drink. Cicadas screamed like electricity in the trees. Under the harsh fluorescent lights, Annabelle wore her armor: purple-streaked hair, thick kohl, chipped black polish. On the inside of her wrist, a moth tattoo lay half-hidden under the cuff of her work shirt—something delicate made permanent, the way she preferred her softness—disguised.

She looked deliberate. Severe. Untouchable.

Beneath it, her beauty was almost antique—soft and luminous, deliberately hidden. She had learned early that visible beauty in Mississippi was not a blessing. It was an invitation.

Dewey Ray Pritchard owned the place. He had never met Phil; Phil had been three owners ago. He managed it the way men manage small inheritances that never quite become fortunes: with routine and stubbornness. He came in before dawn, counted cigarettes, changed out the coffee, complained about gas prices, and watched the world through the bulletproof glass like it was weather.

Annabelle was his best night cashier: honest, unsentimental, and almost never absent. Fever was the only thing that could keep her home, and even then it had to be bad enough to make the walls move. The floor stayed clean. So did the register. Customers who came in looking for trouble usually found themselves contained before they understood how it had happened. In that kind of place, making the job look easy was its own skill.

"You keep making it look like a real business," Dewey Ray told her once, as if she was doing him a favor.

"Aww, thanks, Dewey Ray." Annabelle smiled because it was easier than explaining that order was the only thing she had ever been able to control.

Her mother's name, on paper, was Betsy Smith Crump Davidson Davidson Johnson—an accumulation of men like bad weather patterns. Betsy had been seventeen when Annabelle was born, and romantic enough then to name her after a poem. Hopeless romantic, even now, except romance had started to look a lot like survival and pills and smoke and whatever kept the edges from cutting her.

Ben Crump—Annabelle's father—had fled town when she was two, leaving a string of hot checks and four warrants behind him, as if he'd wanted to be remembered by paperwork.

If Annabelle considered anyone fatherly, it was Sylvester Davidson, only because he had been present the most. For a while he'd been almost decent. At ten, he took her to a few minor league baseball games and let her hold the scorecard like it mattered. At twelve, he taught her to change a tire, the jack trembling in her hands, a lesson meant for the day no one came. By thirteen, he was gone, and she never saw him again.

Al Johnson lasted eight months when Annabelle was fifteen. The in-between times were revolving doors of boyfriends—if you could call them that. Mostly, they were Betsy's connections for weed and meth. Men who came by with their pockets heavy with pills and their eyes empty; men who stayed because Betsy never asked them to leave until she had to.

Love came in moving trucks. Left in slammed doors.

Annabelle stopped believing in permanence.

On nights when the store was slow and the highway went quiet, she would look out at the dark cotton fields beyond the lights. The land didn't move. It waited. It had patience. Mississippi was full of things that waited.

Chapter 2

Celeste Voss arrived from the north.

She never flew. Planes felt like surrender: to turbulence, to crowds, to schedules that weren't hers. She traveled by private coach—black, long, quiet as a promise—and she traveled the way she lived: contained, controlled, discreet, and she could afford it.

The coach rolled down Highway 61 from Memphis with a driver who spoke only when spoken to. Celeste was on her way to New Orleans where she kept a townhouse for southern operations. New Orleans was suitable: old money and newer sins, humidity that softened everything, a city that understood transaction without demanding explanation.

Yazoo City was too small to matter. Too small to sleep in. But they needed diesel, and Celeste had learned to respect detours. They were where you found what wasn't on the map.

"Stop here," she told the driver, as if it were a business decision. Which, for her, it was.

Phil's Fill-R-Ups was a hard rectangle of fluorescent light in a landscape of darkness. The coach eased into the lot with a smoothness that made the other vehicles look embarrassed. A pickup idled near the ice machine. A man in camouflage stared openly, as if the coach had offended him by existing.

Celeste stepped down wearing a black silk blouse and a cream linen blazer—tailored, cool, precise. She dressed for climate the way a strategist plans for terrain. Sleeves rolled once, gold at her throat, no wasted movement.

"I need diesel," she said, voice calm as a contract.

Dewey Ray came out from the back like a man forced into contact with novelty. He looked at the coach the way he might look at a spaceship.

"You'll have to pull forward," he said, as if he were addressing any other vehicle. "Diesel's on the far side."

Celeste nodded and turned toward the window.

And then she looked at Annabelle.

Not at the makeup. Not at the hair. At the bones beneath it. The structure. The hidden symmetry. The way a face could be made plain on purpose.

Celeste operated in New York—Manhattan penthouses, private clubs, discreet arrangements for men who preferred their appetites curated. She collected women the way other people collected art. Not impulsively. Selectively. She saw value where others saw packaging.

"Beauty isn't rare," Celeste said quietly. "Discipline is."

Annabelle met her gaze and did not look away, which was either courage or exhaustion.

Celeste smiled as if she had discovered something.

"Have you ever thought of leaving?" she asked lightly, like it was small talk.

No one had ever asked Annabelle that.

The question landed between them—soft, casual—yet Annabelle felt it open like cotton splitting.

Chapter 3

Annabelle expected the dark living room, the television talking to itself, the sour-sweet air of something burned too long on a spoon. She opened the back door instead.

Betsy was outside.

The sight landed wrong, like a clock chiming at the wrong hour. Her mother sat in a faded lawn chair, barefoot, her knees drawn up, a paperback open in her lap. Not at a romance with a torn cover or a church flyer. It was a thick book with thin paper, its spine creased the way a book only creases when it has been opened and reopened, not merely owned.

The Complete Works of Edgar Allan Poe.

Betsy had her hair twisted up with a pencil, the way she used to do when Annabelle was little, and Betsy still pretended she was the kind of woman who read. Her face looked washed out in the late light, the sharpness of it newly visible, as if something in her had stepped back just far enough to let the bone show.

Annabelle stood on the threshold for a moment, listening. Cicadas. A car somewhere on the highway. The low hum of the refrigerator behind her, steady as a lie.

Betsy didn't look up right away. Her eyes moved slowly along the page, like they were learning the habit again.

"You out here?" Annabelle said.

Betsy turned a page with her thumb. Her nails were bitten down; the cuticles were raw. Small details that told the truth even when everything else tried not to.

"Couldn't breathe in there," Betsy said. Her voice was flat, not slurred, but thin—like she was speaking through cotton. "Too much... stale."

Annabelle stepped onto the porch. The boards gave a small complaint under her boot.

Betsy's gaze lifted then, and for a second it was almost clean. Not happy. Only present.

"What's this?" Annabelle nodded toward the book.

Betsy glanced down at it as if she'd forgotten it was in her hands. "Poe," she said, like it answered itself.

"I know it's Poe."

Betsy's mouth twitched. "Your daddy used to say I only loved the dead ones. Couldn't hurt me no more."

Annabelle didn't answer. She had learned early that silence was sometimes the only way to keep the conversation from sliding into one of Betsy's moods, into tears or laughter or blame. Silence was a gate you held shut with your body.

Betsy kept looking at her, and Annabelle felt the strange discomfort of being seen by someone who usually looked through her. It made her want to step back into the trailer where the old patterns lived.

"Where you been?" Betsy asked.

"Work." Annabelle's voice stayed even. "Phil's."

Betsy's eyes narrowed slightly. "Mm."

Annabelle could hear the question Betsy didn't ask: Did you see Caleb? Did you talk to him? Did he call? Caleb had been around long enough to become part of Betsy's loose catalog of men and threats—another presence to measure, another reason to be suspicious, another excuse to pretend she was protecting her daughter when mostly she was protecting herself.

Annabelle chose a different truth.

"A woman came through the other night," she said. "Real... put together. Not from here."

Betsy's gaze stayed on her, steady. "A woman."

"Yeah."

Betsy's fingers tightened on the book. The paper made a dry sound. "What'd she want?"

"Gas." Annabelle shrugged. "Coffee. Directions."

Betsy's eyes dipped once, briefly, toward Annabelle's chest, her face, the line of her throat—an old mother's inventory done in a second. Annabelle felt it like a hand.

"And?" Betsy said.

"And she asked about me." Annabelle kept her tone casual, like it was nothing, like it was a story about somebody else. "Asked my name. Asked how old I was."

Betsy's expression didn't change, but something in her gaze sharpened, the way a drunk person's attention can suddenly become precise on the wrong detail.

"She ask why your hair's like that?" Betsy said.

Annabelle almost smiled. "No."

Betsy flipped the book closed with one hand and sat forward. The motion was unsteady but deliberate. She was working to stay in the moment.

"What's her name," Betsy said.

"Celeste."

Betsy repeated it under her breath, testing it like a mouthful of liquor. "Celeste."

"She's from New Orleans," Annabelle added, still not asking anything, just laying the facts down one after another like cards.

Betsy leaned back again. Her eyes went past Annabelle, toward the yard, toward the scrubby line of trees, toward whatever road existed in her mind that led out of this place.

"New Orleans," she said. "Of course."

Annabelle waited. It wasn't patience; it was habit. With Betsy, you waited because if you pushed, you'd get performance. If you waited, you might get something true.

Betsy's hand slid over the cover of the book, the title embossed and faded. She looked at Poe as if she'd gone there on purpose. As if she'd needed something old and formal to hold her upright.

"She pretty?" Betsy asked.

Annabelle hesitated only long enough to tell the truth. "Yeah."

Betsy nodded once, like that settled a calculation.

"What'd she say to you."

"She said there might be work." Annabelle kept her eyes on the yard, not on her mother's face. "Not here."

Betsy's laugh came out dry, without pleasure. "Ain't no work here," she said. "Not for a girl like you."

Annabelle's shoulders tightened. She could feel the familiar flare of anger, the old urge to say *Then why did you keep me here*? But anger with Betsy was like throwing a rock into a swamp. It didn't land; it just disappeared.

"She gave me a number," Annabelle said. "Told me to call."

Betsy didn't ask what kind of work because Betsy knew enough not to ask. Or because she didn't want to know. Either way, Annabelle felt the space around the unspoken thing.

Betsy opened the book again, not to read but to have her hands on something that looked like a life. She stared at the page without moving her eyes.

"You ain't asking me," Betsy said finally.

"No," Annabelle said. "I'm not."

Betsy's lips pressed together. Her throat worked like she was swallowing down something bitter. When she spoke again, her voice was quieter—less performance, more fatigue.

"This town will eat you alive if you stay," Betsy said.

The line landed hard because it wasn't dramatic. It wasn't even angry. It was spoken the way you told someone it was going to frost overnight.

Annabelle's stomach tightened. She felt, for a moment, the child inside her trying to decide whether to believe the mother.

Betsy looked up then, and her eyes were not empty in that instant. They were damaged, yes. But awake.

"Don't make my mistakes," Betsy said. "I thought love was a rope. Turns out it's a chain."

Annabelle swallowed. The air smelled like cut grass and old heat. Somewhere in the distance a dog barked incessantly.

"You don't even know her," Annabelle said, and it came out more defensive than she meant.

Betsy's mouth twitched again, almost a smile, almost a wince.

"I know the kind," Betsy said. "Women like that don't offer you nothing for free. But at least they offer." She glanced toward the trailer, toward the sagging roofline, toward the rooms where Betsy disappeared most days. "This place don't offer. It takes."

Annabelle stared at her mother. She wanted to say, *"You're saying this like you care*. She wanted to say, *why now*? But the moment felt fragile. If she touched it too hard it would crumble.

Betsy's gaze drifted downward, to the book, to the printed words. Her fingers trembled faintly. Not from fear. From hunger.

"You go see her," Betsy said, and there it was—permission without being asked, blessing without the shape of one. "You go look. You don't owe this place nothing."

Annabelle's throat burned. She looked away, toward the yard again, because looking at Betsy's face felt like looking directly at a wound.

After a beat, Betsy added, almost casually, as if correcting herself:

"And you don't owe no man neither."

Annabelle thought of Caleb, of the way he smiled when he wanted something, of the way he disappeared for hours and came back like he'd never left. She thought of how quickly affection turned to expectation. She didn't say his name. She didn't give him that weight.

She nodded once.

Betsy picked up the book again and held it closer, like a shield. "What'd she give you," she asked.

Annabelle reached into her pocket and pulled out the folded slip of paper. She held it out.

Betsy took it carefully, like it might bite. She stared at the number, her lips moving as if she might memorize it. She handed it back.

"Put it somewhere safe," Betsy said. "Not in that damn phone where people can get in it. Write it down. Hide it."

Betsy hesitated, then reached out and touched Annabelle's hair, smoothing it once where the purple had grown uneven.

"Maybe wash that out before you go," she said. "Let them see you."

Annabelle didn't answer.

Betsy's hand lingered a second too long, then fell away.

Annabelle tucked it back into her pocket. "Okay."

Betsy leaned back. The lucidity didn't vanish, but it thinned. Already, Annabelle could see the edges of her mother softening, sliding away from the hard outline of the moment.

Betsy looked down at Poe again and read silently, her eyes moving now, slower than before.

Annabelle stood on the porch for a few seconds longer, watching her mother pretend to be the woman she might have been. Then she went inside, closing the screen door gently behind her, as if the sound could break whatever brief, sober thing had happened in the yard.

Chapter 4

The bus rolled into the city just after noon, air thick enough to feel handled. Annabelle stepped down onto the concrete with her duffel slung over her shoulder and felt the heat settle on her collarbones like a second skin.

New Orleans did not look like it did in photographs. It leaned. It sweated. It smelled faintly of sugar and something old underneath it.

Celeste's instructions had been exact. Walk. Do not take a cab. See it.

Annabelle moved through streets that narrowed as they went, iron balconies curving overhead, paint peeling in disciplined layers. A bead of sweat slipped down the back of her neck and she wiped it away absently.

Not watching. That was the first thing she noticed.

They moved in clusters, in pairs, in loose currents along the sidewalks. Shirts open. Linen. Tank tops. Sunglasses. Hands resting casually at the backs of other men. Laughter without scanning. No one measuring her. No one cataloging.

She passed two men standing close, foreheads nearly touching as they argued softly over a map. One brushed the other's arm without thinking. The gesture was unguarded.

It unsettled her.

Not because of what it was. Because of what it wasn't.

No appraisal.

No transaction.

Just ease.

The music grew louder as she crossed toward Bourbon. Bass bleeding through walls. Rainbow flags draped from balconies. Crowds thickening toward the center of something she did not need to reach.

She stopped at the corner of Royal and Dumaine.

Celeste's townhouse stood three stories high, narrow and composed, its shutters painted a green that did not fade into the noise around it. It did not advertise. It did not lean. It held itself upright.

Annabelle pressed the buzzer.

The door opened without question.

Inside, the air was cool and quiet, like stepping underwater.

Celeste stood at the base of the staircase, barefoot, linen trousers, a silk blouse the color of bone. Her expression did not change at the sight of Annabelle.

"You found it," Celeste said.

"Yes, ma'am."

Celeste's mouth tilted slightly. "Don't."

Annabelle stepped fully inside. The door shut. The city noise reduced to a suggestion.

"Did you walk?" Celeste asked.

"Yes."

"Good."

Celeste took Annabelle's duffel without asking and set it against the wall. The entry smelled faintly of citrus and something cleaner beneath it.

"Come upstairs."

The second floor opened into a sitting room with tall windows overlooking Royal. Through the glass, Annabelle could see the movement of men below like a river flowing past stone.

"They're here for the weekend," Celeste said, following her gaze. "They'll be gone by Tuesday."

Annabelle nodded.

"You look surprised," Celeste added.

"I've never seen…" Annabelle stopped.

"Comfort?" Celeste supplied.

Annabelle did not answer.

Celeste crossed the room and poured water from a glass pitcher into two tumblers. She handed one to Annabelle.

"Drink," she said. "The heat will lie to you."

Annabelle drank. The water tasted cold enough to hurt.

"You're early," Celeste said.

"The bus was."

Celeste studied her the way a jeweler studies a stone before cutting it. Not admiring. Assessing structure.

"You understand why I asked you to come now," Celeste said. "You'll find this easier than you think."

Annabelle glanced toward the window again. Two men below kissed briefly, then separated without drama, without looking around to see who had seen.

"So I could see," Annabelle said.

"Yes."

Celeste sat opposite her, crossing one leg over the other.

"This city is not what you think it is," Celeste said. "It's layered. The loudest thing is rarely the most valuable."

Annabelle absorbed that without asking for explanation.

"You notice something?" Celeste asked.

"They're not looking at me."

Celeste's smile was small but genuine. "Correct."

"And they won't."

Celeste let that sit.

"Desire has markets," she continued. "Segmentation. Geography. Loyalty. You are not entering chaos. You are entering structure."

Annabelle's fingers tightened slightly around the glass.

"I'm not asking you to decide today," Celeste said. "I don't take anyone who can't hold consequence."

"I'm twenty-two."

"Yes," Celeste said calmly. "And unformed."

Annabelle flushed, but she did not look away.

Celeste leaned back.

"You need to see scale," she said. "You need to understand that the world is larger than a truck stop and a boy who disappears when he's bored. You want out."

"I want options," Annabelle said.

The name Caleb hovered between them without being spoken.

"Walk with me," Celeste said.

They stepped back onto Royal Street, not toward Bourbon but running alongside it, moving north toward Canal. Celeste spoke; Annabelle watched. Art galleries and antique shops lined the block. A chandelier the size of a carriage hung in one window, and she tried to imagine the ceiling that had once borne its weight. They passed the marble facade of the Louisiana Supreme Court, its palms bending in the soft wind, ceremonial rather than severe.

The crowd thickened, then thinned again. Men moved around them without touch, without pause. No one looked twice. Annabelle felt invisible in a way that did not diminish her. It steadied her. It felt like permission.

Celeste moved easily through it all, free of watching eyes, pursuit, and appraisal.

Power did not always require volume.

They turned on Conti where the noise softened into echo and then turned back onto Chartres to St. Louis Cathedral. Celeste stopped in front of Café Pontalba and gestured toward the wrought-iron balconies overhead.

"You see spectacle," she said. "I see clientele segmentation and revenue variance."

Annabelle almost smiled.

"You are not for everyone," Celeste continued. "That is your leverage."

Celeste walked half a step ahead, sunglasses in place, her pace unhurried but exact. Annabelle adjusted her bag on her shoulder and listened to the rhythm of their heels against the uneven pavement.

Across the street, a man paused in the doorway of a narrow shop. He stood with one shoulder against the brick, eyes lifted as if studying the ironwork overhead. When Celeste laughed, his gaze shifted—not to the balconies, not to the cathedral—but to her mouth.

His phone lifted slightly in his hand, angled once toward the street.

A moment later, he checked his phone and moved on, measured, unremarkable. The street absorbed him the way it absorbed everything.

Another group of men passed them, laughing, one with his arm draped loosely over another's shoulders. The gesture was effortless.

Annabelle watched them go.

"They don't need me," she said.

"No," Celeste agreed. "They don't."

From the open doorway of a gallery they had already passed, a voice carried out, unlowered:

"She's new."

"Yeah."

"Needs work."

The conversation didn't pause. It didn't shift. It continued as they walked on.

They walked back toward the townhouse as the afternoon tilted toward evening. The light shifted gold against brick.

Inside again, Celeste paused at the staircase.

"You're not staying here," she said.

Annabelle blinked. "I just got here."

"Yes."

"Why?"

"Because if you stay, you will confuse atmosphere for opportunity." Celeste's tone remained even. "I want you deliberate."

Annabelle felt the small sting of dismissal. It surprised her.

"You wanted me to see," she said.

"I did."

"And?"

Celeste's gaze sharpened slightly.

"And now you know the difference between hunger and comfort," she said. "You know you are not hunted here. That matters."

Annabelle nodded.

It made sense.

It felt true.

Celeste crossed to the narrow console table and lifted a slim envelope.

"You're flying to Chicago in the morning."

Annabelle didn't move. "Chicago."

"Yes."

"For what?"

"To sit still," Celeste said. "In a city that does not care whether you exist. No one will look at you. No one will want you. You will have a room. You will have an allowance. You will have time. If you still want this after that, you'll call me."

The statement was not invitation. It was calibration.

Celeste handed her the envelope.

"Be ready at six."

❧

Outside, the noise had grown thicker, the music rising into the warm dark. Annabelle stepped into it and felt once again the absence of eyes on her body.

As she walked down Dumaine toward the river, she noticed a moth pendant in a small shop window. It matched the tattoo on her wrist.

"Oh, dat one been speakin' yo' name since before you knew you was comin', chèrie."

She handed the old woman $10, thanked her, and stepped back into the street.

For the first time in her life, she moved through men without being calculated.

It felt like safety.

It also felt like information.

She walked back toward the small hotel Celeste had arranged for the night.

She did not look back.

Chapter 5

The plane banked over water the color of gunmetal steel.

She pressed her forehead to the window and tried to measure the city. The grid ran clean and unbroken to the lake. Buildings stood upright without apology. Buildings upon buildings. Nothing sagged. Nothing leaned.

Chicago did not sprawl. It stood.

When the wheels hit the runway at O'Hare, the landing felt decisive. She watched the men in dark coats stand too quickly, already reaching for briefcases, phones pressed to their ears, before the plane had stopped moving.

The airport was larger than any building she had ever walked through. Glass, steel, movement. Everyone seemed to know where they were going.

Outside, the wind came off the lake with intention. It cut through her jacket as if it had been waiting. She tasted metal in it. The air did not hang; it moved.

Downtown rose in increments. Concrete, glass, angles. Money made visible.

She watched the buildings the way she once watched cotton prices scroll across a small television above the register—trying to understand the numbers without being told the formula.

❧

Annabelle stepped into the lobby of The Drake and slowed without meaning to.

Right in the middle of the room sat a flower arrangement so enormous it looked almost unreal, like something built for a parade float instead of a table. Roses, lilies, flowers she didn't even know the names of spilled outward in every direction. She wondered how many people it must have taken just to carry it inside.

Above it hung chandeliers that seemed as big as the trees back home. Hundreds of tiny lights shimmered through hanging crystals, scattering soft sparks across the marble floor.

Annabelle stood there a moment longer than she meant to, turning slowly, trying not to stare while staring at everything. The whole place felt less like a hotel and more like a palace someone had forgotten to lock.

At the front desk, she gave her name to a young man dressed in a dark suit.

"Yes, Miss Crump, your room is ready," he said as he handed her a key card. "Miss Voss arranged for the corner room. You'll have the lake on two sides."

The next morning, she stepped outside onto Michigan Avenue. The wind from the lake was chilly even on Labor Day weekend.

She walked south down Michigan toward the building that Celeste had written down for her.

As she passed Louis Vuitton, she noticed a security guard standing at the entrance. She wasn't sure if he was there to welcome someone or to keep them out.

Lyle's Family Clothing back home had never needed a guard to decide if you could shop there.

She walked past a Converse Store and a Nike Store. At least she knew those names.

Another two blocks and she passed Burberry. She wasn't sure she'd ever heard of it, but the security guard standing in front could have been the twin of the one at the other store.

Finally, she reached her destination. Two huge lions sat in the front. Annabelle wondered if they were also security.

She didn't know anything about the place. She only knew Celeste had written the name on a card.

The Art Institute of Chicago

Celeste did not send her anywhere accidentally.

The room she entered was quieter than the rest. The walls were pale. The light came from above, diffused, as if filtered for seriousness.

She stopped in front of a painting that looked, at first, like a mistake.

Muted colors. Everything flattened into plane and shape. Annabelle stood before Still Life with Fruit and a Stringed Instrument and felt the room tilt. A violin lay there, but not as a violin—its curved wood interrupted by a shadow that did not obey gravity. A bowl of fruit hovered in suggestion rather than weight. A bottle collapsed into geometry. The table refused to sit level. Nothing rested where it should, and yet nothing had fallen.

She leaned closer.

The placard read:

Georges Braque.

Oil on canvas.

1938.

The year startled her more than the image.

Nineteen thirty-eight.

The painting did not feel preserved; it felt taken apart.

She searched for the violin again and located it only by memory of being told it existed. Once identified, it dissolved back into an arrangement—curve, becoming a line, a line becoming an interruption.

She stepped away.

No one else seemed disoriented. A man in a dark wool coat stood with his hands clasped behind him, posture composed, studying the canvas as though it were an argument he intended to win. A woman beside him inclined her head in slow affirmation, as if confirming a private thesis.

The instrument suggested a violin only in the most elementary sense—curve where a curve should be, a narrowing where a neck might exist. It was recognition reduced to outline. And even that outline seemed to stray, as if drawn by an impatient hand unwilling to stay within its own borders.

She walked into the next gallery. There a painting hung that was simply a white field and colored geometric shapes stacked upon one another that purported to be a football player. *Painterly realism of a Football Player – Kazimir Malevich* the plaque declared. On the wall across from it hung a work that was simply two vertical bands, one cobalt, one ash. A third—nothing but a single line running across the middle as if someone had tested the brush and stopped.

She stood there longer than she intended.

Color hardened. Perspective fractured. Rectangles became people. A woman's face separated into planes that did not reassemble. A violin became geometry. A horizon refused to lie flat. A railway crossing in flat colored bars, the rails running at angles that ignored the ground beneath them. She waited for the joke to reveal itself.

It did not.

She felt the faintest irritation.

She looked around.

Celeste had sent her here.

Not to admire.

To observe.

The question was not whether the paintings were beautiful. It was whether she understood the system that defined beauty.

Not confused now. Learning the terms of the room.

The names on the wall mattered. The dates mattered. The museum mattered.

The paintings held because everyone agreed they should.

She thought of land appraisals. Of neighborhoods that rose in value because someone with authority declared them "historic." Of numbers becoming real because they were repeated by enough men in suits. Of Caleb Rush, who was somebody in Yazoo City because enough people agreed he was, and nobody had ever thought to ask why.

The violin in the painting did not have to resemble a violin.

It had to participate in a conversation powerful enough to endure.

No one was smirking. They stood in contemplation. A young couple debated "intent." A woman with a museum badge spoke softly about "reduction," "gesture," and "the refusal of illusion." A small plaque noted that many of Braque's works had once been rejected and now traveled internationally.

Rejected. Now revered.

It didn't matter whether she liked the painting. What mattered was that everyone in the room had already agreed it was important.

The seventeenth-century grapes were beautiful because they resembled grapes. But they were also here because someone had said they belonged.

A bale was worth what the market agreed it was worth that morning.

She had seen numbers become truth simply because they were repeated.

A faint, steady calm replaced the irritation.

Reputation. Status. Desire.

Even virtue.

She felt no sudden revelation. No swelling appreciation.

She moved slowly now. Not searching for beauty.

Studying the mechanisms.

By the time she reached the final gallery, she was no longer intimidated.

She was observing.

Annabelle walked outside and stopped next door at Millennium Park.

People were everywhere, many of them gathered around some enormous, shiny silver bean. At least, that's what one of the onlookers had called it.

She sat down and thought.

Inside, the museum assigned worth to color fields and fractured faces.

Outside, some clothing stores were valuable enough to need someone standing guard.

All of it because someone—no, everyone had decided that these things were valuable.

As she stood to go, she did not feel enlightened.

On the walk back to the Drake, she stopped inside the Nike store and picked up a pair of shoes.

She turned one over in her hands.

They cost more than any pair she had ever owned.

No one stood guard at the door.

She brought them to the register.

The cashier didn't look at her.

Not at the shoes. Not at her.

Just scanned. Bagged. Moved on.

The number sat on the receipt—clean, final.

No hesitation. No discussion.

She glanced back at the wall.

Rows of the same shoe. Stacked. Repeated.

Still worth what they said it was.

She folded the receipt once.

Chapter 6

Betsy hugged her too tight when she stepped through the door.

Too tight and too bright.

"You look thinner," Betsy said, pulling back just enough to inspect her face, as if New Orleans had taken something visible.

Annabelle smelled something. It wasn't liquor. That might have been better. Something metallic under powder. Something like heat.

Then she saw it.

High on Betsy's shoulder, just beneath the collarbone. Yellow at the edges. Deepening purple at the center. The imprint of four fingers and the beginning of a thumb.

The mark did not shock her.

It irritated her.

"Mama."

"What."

Annabelle did not point. "You fall?"

Betsy's laugh came too fast. "I ain't falling nowhere."

The kitchen hummed. Refrigerator. Clock. The faint rattle of the window unit fighting the humidity.

Silence pressed in.

"He just grabbed me," Betsy added, adjusting the strap of her tank top without quite covering the bruise. "Don't make it into something."

He.

Not a name.

Annabelle let her bag rest against the wall.

Five days ago she had stood in a quiet room on Royal Street and listened to a woman describe consent as architecture. Something you built first. Something that held.

Now she stood in a kitchen that smelled like burned plastic and saw what happened when nothing was built at all.

"Does he live here," she asked.

Betsy turned toward the sink, rinsing a mug that didn't need rinsing. "For now."

For now.

That was the answer. Temporary. Always temporary. Long enough to leave damage.

Annabelle stepped closer, not to inspect the bruise, but to see Betsy's eyes.

They were clear.

Clear enough to choose.

That unsettled her more than intoxication would have.

"You hungry?" she asked. "I got some chicken."

Annabelle looked around the room. A pair of boots near the back door. Not expensive. Mud still in the treads. A belt looped over the back of a chair. Male weight without male presence.

"Where is he."

"Out."

Another non-answer.

Outside, the afternoon lay flat over the fields. Cotton stood still in ordinary light. No wind. No movement. Nothing mystical. Just rows and waiting.

Annabelle looked at the bruise again.

Betsy reached for the mug beside the sink. Her hand shook just enough to make it tap once against the counter.

Neither of them mentioned it.

Chapter 7

Annabelle did not leave.

Not immediately.

She had roots—not sentimental, but heavy. Mississippi held her through gravity, expectation, and boys who never stopped thinking she was theirs.

Caleb Rush was one of them. Three weeks in tenth grade. In Yazoo City, which meant something faster than the word dating implied: hands on her waist in the hallway, his friends calling her his girl, evenings spent in his pickup on a dirt road, a possessiveness disguised as pride.

It ended. He didn't.

Now he lingered at Phil's Fill-R-Ups at night, watching the coach when it returned, watching Celeste, watching Annabelle as if he could reclaim something by staring long enough. Moths and mosquitoes hummed around the nightwatcher outside, each circling the cold light for a different reason.

"You think you're better than us?" he asked one night, leaning on the counter like the store belonged to him.

Annabelle scanned his energy drink, slid it toward him, and kept her face blank.

Caleb didn't take it.

His hand came across the counter instead, turning her wrist slightly—just enough to bring the moth into view.

"You still got this thing."

Annabelle didn't pull back right away.

Then she did.

"Don't."

He smiled, like she'd said something familiar instead of serious.

"Relax."

Celeste stood near the coffee station, unhurried, as if time had been built around her. She looked at Caleb once—no hostility, no fear—only a flat assessment, the way you might regard weather.

Caleb's jaw tightened. He wanted a reaction. He wanted proof that he existed in her world.

Celeste gave him nothing.

She returned every week from New Orleans, always leaving before dawn: fuel, coffee, conversation. Sometimes she asked Dewey Ray about diesel prices, pretending she cared. Sometimes she watched Annabelle with an attention that made the store feel too bright.

Books began appearing in Annabelle's locker—history, strategy, art, reinvention. No note. No message. Just offerings, like bribes or invitations.

"You are not prey," Celeste said one night, as if she were stating a fact Annabelle had forgotten.

"And what are you?" Annabelle asked.

"Practical," Celeste replied.

By late September, the cotton was swollen and ready. The fields glowed under the moon like something alive and waiting to be cut open.

And they did not like the coach.

Once, walking home, Annabelle felt cotton brush her wrist where no field stood. Possession had many forms. The land had raised her. It did not intend to surrender her easily.

Chapter 8

Caleb crossed the road one night—not drunk, not loud, just there.

Annabelle had clocked out. The store lights burned behind her. The highway thinned into dark ahead. The air carried damp soil and diesel. Cicadas scraped the trees. A dog barked once, then fell silent.

He stepped into her path.

"You been talking to her," he said.

She kept walking until he matched her pace.

He caught her wrist—the moth pressed flat beneath his thumb—and the wind dropped.

It had been moving steadily through the rows, a low push from west to east. Now it stopped. The field stilled mid-breath.

"You don't get to leave," he said.

His grip tightened. Heat gathered under his fingers. She could feel his pulse, quick and careless.

She did not look at him. She looked past him, into the pale geometry of the rows.

"I am not yours," she said.

He shifted to block her. A small movement. Habit more than threat.

His heel found the softened edge where the ditch met the first row. The ground gave way under his weight. He tried to correct it, stepping forward instead of back.

The first plants shook. White flashed in the moonlight.

He windmilled once, startled. His other foot slid deeper between the stems. The soil there had been watered that afternoon; it held no resistance. His shoulder drove into the stalks. Cotton burst against his shirt, splitting, shedding.

The wind came back hard.

Rows bent in one direction, then another. From the road it looked like a single motion, a long pale fold.

He went down hard into the row. The plants closed over him faster than she expected. The cotton was taller than it looked from the road.

He made a short sound.

Then he went down fully into the row.

The disturbance moved outward in a tight circle—three, maybe four plants—then settled. Stems righted themselves unevenly. White bolls rocked and grew still.

The wind continued across the rest of the field as if nothing had interrupted it.

Annabelle stood in the road. Her wrist cooled where he had held it.

She waited for him to rise swearing.

He did not.

She listened for movement. Heard none.

Her breathing slowed. Her heart steadied.

She did not step into the field.
She turned and walked home.

Chapter 9

Annabelle returned to New Orleans with the unsigned contract in her bag.

The city met her with heat and music and the sweet rot of old stones sweating under sun. She walked past voodoo shops in the French Quarter—gris-gris, candles, painted saints and sinners—things that promised power for a price. All watched. None touched her.

But Mississippi had sent a message.

Celeste received her in linen again, charcoal this time—tailored, spare, expensive. The townhouse smelled faintly of citrus and something floral that never quite became perfume. The marble table in the sitting room looked like it had never held anything messy.

"You look different," Celeste observed.

"I am," Annabelle replied.

Celeste studied her the way she had studied her at the window in Yazoo City. Not her hair or makeup. Her bones.

"Did you say goodbye?" Celeste asked.

"Yes."

"And did it resist?"

Annabelle met her eyes.

"Not anymore."

Celeste's mouth softened into something like approval and nothing like affection.

The contract lay on the marble: education, relocation to New York, an apartment, earnings unmatched by her town, and a sentence Celeste had included with deliberate precision:

No one touches you without your consent.

Annabelle read it twice anyway. She had learned early that words could be used like doors: to let you in, or to lock you out.

"And when I'm done?" she asked.

Celeste leaned back slightly, as if the question amused her.

"You won't be," she said.

Annabelle could hear it, then—the true offer beneath the offer. It wasn't rescue. It wasn't romance, not even her body—her future.

She picked up the pen.

Outside, New Orleans kept humming. Somewhere, a siren rose and fell and disappeared into the heat. The city did not care what she signed. The city cared only that she understood what she was buying.

Annabelle signed.

Ink decisive.

Mississippi did not rumble. New Orleans did not flare. But somewhere far north, in a Manhattan apartment Celeste had not yet offered, the air shifted slightly—making room.

Chapter 10

Three days later, Annabelle watched Manhattan assemble itself beyond the airplane window—grids, steel, compression. No horizon. No cotton fields rupturing in white, no sky wide enough to swallow a person whole. Manhattan rose instead, unapologetic and entire.

The air outside LaGuardia smelled faintly of jet fuel and hot pavement. Cars moved in narrow lanes like pieces in a puzzle already solved. No one hesitated.

Celeste was waiting at the curb outside baggage claim, exactly as if she had always been there.

When the car let them out on Lexington, the sidewalk moved faster than she expected. Men in suits walked with phones pressed to their ears. A delivery cyclist threaded between taxis without looking up. No one stopped unless they had already decided to.

"Slow down," she said. "You left Mississippi. You don't have to prove anything to the sidewalk."

Annabelle adjusted, matching Celeste's unhurried pace, feeling the city's rhythm press against her ribs.

The townhouse on the Upper East Side was narrow, pale stone, restrained. No ornamental excess.

The doorman across the street glanced at them once and then deliberately looked away, the way men do when they recognize a building that prefers discretion.

When the heavy door closed behind her, Annabelle felt a small gravity settle into her chest. East Seventy-Sixth and Park Avenue.

The townhouse felt less like a home than an office designed for discretion.

"Park Avenue doesn't receive girls named for cotton farmers," Celeste said. "It receives women with names that suggest they were educated somewhere expensive."

Annabelle did not flinch. “What would you suggest?”

"Langford," Celeste said, as if testing the weight of it. She shook her head slightly. "Respectable. But respectable is ordinary dressed up." She was quiet for a moment. "Sinclair. Cleaner. Suggests money that doesn't need to explain itself."

She studied Annabelle's face the way she had studied it through the window at Phil's Fill-R-Ups.

"No," she said finally. "Neither of them fits the bones."

Another silence.

"Devereaux," she said.

She let it settle in the room.

"Belle Devereaux. It suggests you were born somewhere that required manners and lost something that required recovery. That's the right kind of history for this address."

Annabelle considered the syllables. “It isn’t mine.”

“Nothing here is,” Celeste replied. “That’s the point.”

Inside there was symmetry. Quiet art. Walls bare of sentiment. Even the air felt filtered, silent.

"You're not here to become someone else," Celeste said, handing her a glass of water—cold, plain, precise. "You're here to become precise."

Annabelle nodded, the glass cool against her palm. She understood precision.

From the guest room window, she watched the city move below—yellow taxis threading between headlights, a food cart closing for the night while a man in a white apron sprayed the sidewalk clean. Steam drifted from a grate and disappeared between two buildings before it reached the sky.

In Yazoo City, someone was always looking.

Here, no one cared who she had been.

That was not freedom.

It was opportunity.

Chapter 11

The coffee place was three blocks north on Lexington, the kind of narrow shop that had no sign visible from the street, only a small chalkboard in the window listing two options. She had passed it the day before with Celeste and filed it without meaning to.

Inside, two men in suits stood at the counter without speaking, phones face-down beside their cups. A woman in running clothes paid without looking up from whatever she was reading on her phone. Nobody made eye contact. Nobody performed friendliness. The transaction happened in under a minute and everyone moved on.

Outside, Lexington was already in full motion. Not chaotic—directed. Every person on the sidewalk seemed to know not just where they were going but exactly how long it would take to get there. A bus compressed its brakes at the corner and four people boarded without breaking stride. A man in a dark coat walked against the flow without anyone adjusting for him, the crowd parting and closing around him like water.

Belle stood on the sidewalk with her coffee and watched.

In Yazoo City, you could tell a stranger by the way they walked. Here everyone walked like a stranger, and nobody noticed anyone else. The anonymity was not cold. It was architectural. The city had been built for exactly this—ten thousand private lives moving through the same space without collision, without obligation, without anyone requiring anything of anyone they hadn't agreed to in advance.

She turned south toward the townhouse.

The wind came off the park two blocks west and moved through the cross streets in cold, clean pulses. She felt it against her face and did not look away from it.

She was beginning to understand the city.

It did not care about her history.

That was not indifference.

That was the offer.

❧

A woman named Evelyn Carr arrived the following Tuesday at precisely ten. Gray suit. Unadorned pearls. A leather folio that looked older than Annabelle. She moved through the townhouse the way certain older women move—as if the room had been arranged for her convenience and she was simply confirming it.

Celeste made the introduction without ceremony.

"Evelyn corrects governors," she said. "And occasionally their wives."

Then she left the room.

Evelyn set the folio on the dining table without opening it. She studied Annabelle the way a pianist studies a piano in an unfamiliar room—not unkindly, but with the detached attention of someone assessing an instrument before committing to it.

She did not smile.

"Say 'pen,'" she said.

Annabelle did.

Evelyn's expression did not change.

"Again."

"Pen."

The word came out the way it always had. The way it had come out in every classroom, every conversation, every transaction at the truck stop. It was a word she had never once thought about.

"Not 'pin,'" Evelyn said evenly. "Pen."

Annabelle felt the correction land somewhere behind her teeth. Not embarrassment exactly. Something older than embarrassment. The particular shame of discovering that something you learned before you could think about learning—the shape of a vowel, the weight of a syllable—had been wrong the entire time. That the voice you had carried out of Mississippi was already marked before you opened your mouth.

She tried again, moving the vowel further back in her throat.

"Pe—n."

"Hold the e," Evelyn instructed. "Do not let it collapse."

Annabelle held it.

The word felt strange in her mouth. Formal. Like wearing someone else's coat and finding it fit better than your own.

"Again."

By the sixth repetition something shifted. The word separated itself from childhood. It became a sound she was making deliberately rather than one she had simply inherited.

She was not sure yet whether that was progress or loss.

They worked for two hours at the dining table beneath a chandelier that hummed faintly in the afternoon heat. Vowels isolated, examined, rebuilt. Consonants released from the back of the throat and brought forward. Evelyn never raised her voice. She corrected the way a surgeon corrects—precisely, without drama, without apology.

At one point Annabelle stopped mid-word.

"I sound like someone else," she said.

Evelyn looked at her steadily.

"You sound like someone who has options," she replied.

That sat differently than Annabelle expected.

"Do not erase where you are from," Evelyn continued. "Control when it appears. There is a difference between hiding something and deciding when to show it."

Annabelle thought of the moth tattoo beneath her cuff. Something delicate made permanent. Softness disguised.

She had understood that principle long before this room.

They practiced silence next.

"Count to two before answering," Evelyn instructed. "Three if the question is personal."

"Why?"

Evelyn's mouth tilted slightly.

"You just answered in less than one," she said. "That is why."

❧

Evelyn Carr left at noon.

Celeste did not ask for a report. She had been listening from the hallway.

“Good,” she said, as if confirming a delivery had arrived intact. “We’ll proceed.”

Clothing came next.

Not shopping.

Assessment.

Annabelle's suitcase was opened on the bed in the guest room. Celeste removed each item without commentary. Black denim. A ribbed tank. Two fitted dresses with cutouts at the waist. A cardigan that had once been soft but now held the faint fatigue of Mississippi humidity.

They were not ugly. They were declarative.

Celeste made two piles.

❧

The smaller remained on the bed.

The larger went back into the suitcase.

"You are not dressing to attract," Celeste said. "You are dressing to be assessed."

She lifted a fitted dress between two fingers.

"This announces need."

It joined the discard pile.

"What you will wear must suggest that access to you is selective and temporary."

There was no anger in it. No critique of taste. Only utility.

"The hair," Celeste said.

❧

That afternoon a car took them uptown to a salon that did not advertise. The receptionist did not blink at the purple.

The stylist examined it clinically.

"We'll have to lift it twice. Maybe three visits to settle it properly."

Annabelle sat for three hours while the color was stripped in stages. The chemical scent filled her nose. Foils crackled. Heat pressed down. The purple bled into the sink like something wounded.

The first gloss came back too warm. They sent her home and started again the following week. The second came back too flat—something vital had been removed without replacement.

By the third visit the shade finally held. A deep, almost black, brown. Not romantic. Not glossy. Structured.

When they turned the chair, she looked startlingly younger.

And unshielded.

Celeste studied her reflection rather than her face.

"Better," she said. "Now you are a question."

❧

The following morning, the tailor arrived.

He introduced himself as Mr. Armand and spoke almost exclusively in numbers. Shoulders squared. Spine straight. He measured from the nape to the waist, from the waist to the hip, and from the hip to the knee. The tape slid cold against the hollow of her back.

“Stand naturally,” he said.

She did not know what that meant anymore.

Celeste selected fabrics from a leather-bound book.

Charcoal wool. Midnight silk. Bone crepe. Navy that was almost black.

“No prints,” Celeste said. “No texture that reads seasonal. Nothing that suggests you chose it because you liked it.”

Mr. Armand pinned a muslin jacket along her sides, drawing it in until her posture corrected itself.

“Clothing should instruct the body,” Celeste said. “Not decorate it.”

He marked the waist half an inch higher than she was used to. Lengthened hemlines just below the knee. Sleeves to the wrist bone.

"No cleavage," Celeste said. "No apology."

They reduced her to essentials in silence:

Three dresses.

Two tailored jackets.

Four blouses in silk that did not cling.

One coat in camel hair.

Shoes with a modest heel, never stiletto.

"Height must look structural," Celeste said. "Not aggressive."

Jewelry was next.

Celeste removed Annabelle's moth pendant and placed it in a drawer.

"For now." The drawer closed with a soft click.

Outside, a truck passed on Seventy-Sixth Street. The sound arrived a half second late, as if the building had briefly held its breath. Belle stood very still. The room felt the same as it had a moment before—same light, same filtered air, same quiet art on the walls.

But something in it had gone slightly less certain.

She did not mention it.

A single gold chain replaced it. No charm.

"Expensive," Celeste said, "but unspecific."

Afternoons became choreography.

How to sit without folding inward.

How to cross her legs without clutching.

How to remove a coat slowly enough that it implied patience. How to hold a glass by the stem, not the bowl.

They practiced entering a room.

"Pause in the doorway," Celeste instructed. "Allow the room to register you before you register it."

They practiced silence again.

"If you answer too quickly, you lower yourself. Let them lean forward."

Meals were instruction as well.

Fork placement.

Bread torn, never bitten.

Wine sipped, never swallowed.

"Neutrality," Celeste repeated, "is wealth."

The accent softened. The hair darkened. The clothing narrowed her into clean lines. The posture lengthened her.

By the end of the three weeks, she no longer recognized the girl who would have laughed too quickly, spoken too fast, filled silence with explanation.

Celeste watched her across the dining table one evening.

"Say 'pen.'"

"Pen."

The vowel held.

Celeste nodded once.

"What we are doing," she said, "is not improvement. It is translation."

Annabelle looked at her reflection in the darkened window. The girl from Yazoo City had not vanished.

She had been reorganized.

Like the violin in the painting.

Taken apart.

Reassembled according to different rules.

Nothing visible had been added.

Everything essential had been measured.

And for the first time, Annabelle understood that refinement was not about beauty.

It was about control.

Chapter 12

The irregularity first appeared six months earlier.

Three wire transfers had been flagged by internal compliance. Identical amounts, spaced precisely thirty days apart. Predictable. Structured. The recipient, Easton Advisory Partners, LLC, had been incorporated ten years ago. There were no service agreements on file. No invoices. No engagement codes.

Thomas Halbrecht did not panic. As the firm's founding partner, panic had never been useful to him.

He calculated.

His partner, Daniel Pierce, was meticulous in visible matters. If he had authorized recurring payments, they were deliberate.

A recurring event implied an arrangement.

An arrangement, in turn, established liability.

Halbrecht had requested documentation quietly.

Hotel folios had been pulled through accounting. Car service logs were routed through assistants who believed they were reconciling travel. Calendar entries marked "private dinner" with no client designation.

The pattern was not geographic.

It was temporal.

Every thirty days, within a seventy-two-hour window, Pierce's evenings went dark.

His calendar showed no firm events, recorded dinners, or charitable boards.

Halbrecht hired a firm.

"Discreet," he said. "No contact. I want correlation."

The firm assigned two operatives.

Within a week, they had expanded from the only corporate breadcrumb Pierce had left behind—a car service invoice routed once through his assistant.

From there, dispatch logs revealed recurring pickups within identical time windows.

Hotel merchant codes, extracted from incidental charges that had slipped through the reimbursement process, led them to two properties. Security videos confirmed the pattern.

Clean.

Deliberate.

They had photographs.

Lobby security stills.

A private elevator bank.

A young woman entering twelve minutes after Pierce.

Thomas had studied the image.

Not the hotel.

Not the timing.

The woman.

Young. Controlled. Arriving alone.

That interested him.

This was not just about indiscretion.

Thomas closed the folder—and waited.

Chapter 13

Celeste did not mention the apartment until the third week.

"You'll be moving tomorrow," she said, closing a folder.

"Where?" Annabelle asked.

"A few blocks away. 75th between Madison and Park. Two-bedroom. Leased through an intermediary."

There was no discussion of preference.

The building had a doorman who did not ask questions and an elevator that did not hesitate between floors.

Angelique opened the door.

She was beautiful without softness—deep, even skin as dark as a moonless midnight, cheekbones cut cleanly, posture already composed.

"You're early," she said, which Annabelle later understood meant on time.

The apartment was narrow but exact. Neutral furniture. No photographs. Two identical bedrooms at opposite ends of the hall.

"Celeste prefers pairing," Angelique said. "Less noise. Fewer variables."

Annabelle placed her suitcase on the bed.

Angelique watched without intrusion.

"You don't bring clients here," Angelique said. "Ever."

"Understood."

"The building believes we work in events."

"Understood."

Angelique nodded once.

"If you're late, you text me. If I'm late, I text you. If something feels wrong, you leave."

She did not elaborate.

The closet was already measured. Hangers spaced evenly. Shoes aligned.

Annabelle realized the apartment was not shared space.

That night, she lay awake listening to the city instead of cicadas. Horns and distant voices—sounds that belonged to no one.

Angelique did not speak through the wall.

Chapter 14

Belle woke to machinery.

Not to the sounds of a Mississippi morning: alarm clocks, birds, cicadas building voltage in the trees.

Machinery.

The city began before she did—buses compressing air at the curb, delivery trucks idling beneath her window, the metallic complaint of a gate rolling upward somewhere below. Even at six-thirty, Manhattan did not stretch. It advanced.

Angelique was already in the kitchen.

The apartment was narrow enough that sound carried. Cabinet. Mug. Running water. Silence again.

Belle stood in the doorway for a moment before entering, calibrating.

Angelique did not greet her. She did not ignore her either. She sat at the counter closest to the sink, straight-backed, her hair tied back, gripping a white mug in both hands as if holding on to its warmth required focus.

"Morning," Belle said.

Angelique inclined her head slightly. "You're adjusting."

It was not a question.

Belle poured coffee into the second mug—black, unsweetened. The refrigerator had already been divided without discussion. Left shelf. Right shelf. Two separate cartons of eggs. Two separate bottles of water. Nothing labeled. Nothing borrowed.

In Mississippi, the refrigerator had been a scene of communal chaos—leftovers without dates, milk questionable, something metallic in the air.

They moved around each other carefully, not touching. The bathroom schedule had resolved itself by the third day. Belle earlier. Angelique later. The mirror was wiped clean after each use. Towels hung precisely. No cosmetics left open.

The rules had not been spoken.

They had been observed.

At night, Belle lay in bed and listened to Angelique's measured steps in the hallway—heel, pause, heel. The rhythm was controlled, almost rehearsed. Once, the door closed at 9:12 p.m. Another night at 11:03. Never slammed. Never careless.

Belle did not ask where she went.

Angelique did not ask either.

Calls to Mississippi became shorter.

Betsy spoke in fragments now. Weather. A neighbor's dog. There was always a television in the background, too loud. A laugh that arrived half a second late.

"You sound busy," Betsy said once.

"I am," Belle answered.

It felt like a betrayal to say it calmly.

After hanging up, she would sit at the small kitchen table and stare at the two place settings across from each other. Two women building independence in parallel rooms. One leaving a house that leaned. One refusing to lean.

She missed the stillness of fields in late summer—the way cotton held light without motion.

She did not miss being watched.

Independence did not feel triumphant.

It felt procedural.

In the mornings, Angelique's presence steadied the apartment. In the evenings, her absence defined it.

The apartment would grow quiet after dinner.

Belle sometimes sat there longer than necessary, the overhead light pooling on the table the way late sun used to sit on the cotton fields.

Chapter 15

Celeste did not rush deployment.

For another two weeks, Annabelle went nowhere of consequence.

She dined at empty tables before service began. Practiced ordering without apology. Practiced declining dessert without explanation.

"Again," Celeste would say.

The first rehearsal ended early.

"You're speaking too quickly," Celeste said. "You are not auditioning."

The second ended because Annabelle reached for her glass before the waiter stepped away.

"Wait," Celeste said. "You move after the room moves."

By the end of the second week, the corrections grew smaller.

She learned which fork to ignore. Which wine to sip without preference. How long to hold eye contact without invitation.

There were evenings when nothing happened at all.

Celeste read at the head of the table. Annabelle sat opposite, saying nothing unless addressed.

Silence was no longer absence.

It was placement.

The wardrobe narrowed her into uniform.

Navy. Bone. Black.

The third navy dress felt indistinguishable from the second.

That was the point.

"You are not here to be remembered," Celeste said once. "You are here to be selected."

By the third week, Annabelle could enter a room without scanning it.

She allowed others to notice first.

❧

The meal rehearsals happened at a restaurant on Sixty-Third Street that did not open until seven. Celeste had an arrangement with the maître d' that allowed them the room between five and six-thirty, before the evening's actual guests arrived. The tables were already set. The lighting was already low. A single waiter named Marcus moved through the room with the particular patience of someone being paid to simulate normalcy.

The third rehearsal was the one that mattered.

They had ordered. The food had arrived. Belle was managing the conversation Celeste had constructed—a hedge fund manager, a foundation dinner, a piece of sculpture he had recently acquired—when Marcus returned to refill her water glass.

She looked up at him.

Just briefly. Just the instinctive acknowledgment of someone entering her peripheral space.

Marcus refilled the glass and withdrew.

Celeste set her fork down.

"What did you just do," she said.

Belle considered. "I looked at him."

"Why."

"He came close. It was instinct."

"Yes," Celeste said. "And instinct is Mississippi."

Belle felt the correction land somewhere precise and unwelcome.

"He's a person," she said.

Celeste looked at her steadily.

"Yes," she said. "And in this room, at this table, his personhood is not the point. Your composure is." She lifted her fork again. "He is part of the room. You acknowledge the room once, when you enter it. After that it moves around you. Not the other way."

Belle picked up her own fork.

"That seems unkind," she said.

Celeste tilted her head slightly. Not irritation. Something more like interest.

"Kindness," she said, "is a private transaction. This is a professional one. Marcus understands the distinction. He is counting on you to understand it too."

Belle looked at her plate.

"Try again," Celeste said.

Marcus appeared at the edge of the room with a breadbasket.

This time Belle did not look up.

The basket was placed and removed without acknowledgment.

The conversation resumed.

After a moment Celeste said, quietly, as if noting something in passing:

"Better."

❧

Evelyn returned the following Thursday.

Same gray suit. Same unadorned pearls. The leather folio open this time, a single page of handwritten notes inside it that Belle could not read from across the table.

They had been working for forty minutes—consonants, the particular flatness of certain vowels that Evelyn called *regional collapse*—when Belle stopped mid-sentence.

"Why does it matter," she said.

Evelyn looked at her without expression.

"The accent," Belle continued. "You can hear the intelligence regardless."

"Can you," Evelyn said.

"Yes."

Evelyn closed the folio.

"Tell me, "she said, "what you hear when a man speaks with a strong regional accent in a room full of men who do not."

Belle considered that honestly.

She thought of Dewey Ray. Of the men at the counter at Phil's. Of the particular way certain voices were heard and certain voices were filed away before they finished their sentences.

She did not answer.

"You hear it," Evelyn said. "You make a calculation in under a second. You are not cruel about it. You are simply efficient." She opened the folio again. "The men in the rooms you are entering will do the same. They will not know they are doing it. That is worse, not better." She looked at Belle directly. "I am not asking you to be ashamed of where you are from. I am asking you to choose when it enters the room."

Belle sat with that for a moment.

"And if I don't want to choose," she said. "If I want it to enter whenever it enters."

Evelyn's expression did not change.

"Then you will spend a great deal of energy managing other people's calculations instead of your own." She paused. "That is also a choice. I simply don't recommend it."

She turned to the page in the folio.

"Again," she said. "From the beginning."

Belle began again.

This time the word held differently. Not because she had erased anything. Because she had decided.

That was what Evelyn had been waiting for.

She did not say so.

She simply turned the page.

Chapter 16

Celeste did not conduct daily instruction.

She delegated.

Leila arrived first. She was corn-fed beautiful—the kind that came from flat land and good bones and generations of people who worked outdoors and didn't know they were striking. Tall without apology, dark blonde hair pulled back with the casual authority of a woman who had stopped thinking about it years ago. She looked like the girl who had been homecoming queen in some small Ohio town, left and never looked back, and become something the town didn't have a name for.

Sharp eyes, sharper mouth, a voice that never rose but cut cleanly through pretense. She had the kind of stillness that made other people aware of their own noise. Within ten minutes of sitting across from Belle, she had identified three things Belle did not know about herself.

"You're not charming," Leila said.

Belle felt the statement land.

"You're deliberate," Leila continued. "That's rarer. Charm is available everywhere. Every pretty girl from anywhere has charm. Deliberate is something else entirely."

She leaned forward slightly.

"Stop trying to be the first thing. Use the second."

The lesson was not seduction. It was containment.

They practiced conversation at the dining table for two hours. Neutral topics. Art. Travel. Markets. Belle had opinions about all of them—or believed she did—and discovered quickly that opinions were not what was being asked for.

"You're filling space," Leila said.

"I'm answering the question."

"No," Leila said. "You're performing. There's a difference."

Belle tried again.

This time she waited.

The silence stretched long enough to become uncomfortable.

Leila smiled for the first time.

"There," she said. "Now he leans forward. Now the conversation belongs to you."

Belle felt the distinction settle somewhere precise and permanent. Not the lesson itself—the sensation of the room shifting when she stopped filling it.

"Nothing personal," Leila continued, "unless you intend it as a weapon. Nothing political unless you've been invited into the argument. Discretion is not silence. It's filtration."

She stood to leave.

"You'll get it wrong the first few times," she added at the door. "That's fine. Just notice when you do."

Mei was the kind of beautiful that arrived quietly and stayed. Fine-boned, precise, her black hair cut bluntly at the jaw in a way that suggested she had decided on it once and never reconsidered. Her eyes were completely still—the eyes of someone who had long ago decided that watching was more useful than speaking. She came the following week.

She did not speak for the first twenty minutes.

She simply sat across from Belle in the townhouse sitting room and watched. She wasn't rude or cold. Simply patient—her total attention that of someone reading a text in a language they already knew.

Belle felt herself begin to fidget. She stopped. Fidgeted again.

Mei noticed.

She said nothing.

They went to lunch at a restaurant on Madison that Mei chose without explanation. They were seated and Mei ordered water and then went quiet again, watching the room.

After several minutes she said, almost to herself: "The man by the window. Second from the left."

Belle looked.

"His phone is face down," Belle said.

Mei shook her head slightly.

"Look again."

Belle looked.

The phone was face up. The watch was last season. The shoes were impeccable.

"He's performing wealth," Mei said quietly. "The shoes are real. Everything else is effort."

Belle studied him.

"How do you know the shoes are real?"

"Because that's where men who grew up with money spend it first," Mei said. "Shoes and watches. In that order. Everything else is decoration."

She sipped her water.

"A man who grew up without it buys the watch first. Bigger. Louder. Something people see before they see his feet."

Belle looked at the man again with different eyes.

"What else?" she asked.

Mei almost smiled.

"That's the right question," she said.

They stayed for two hours.

Belle did not speak much.

For the first time since arriving in New York, that felt like exactly the correct amount.

Her first solo appointment was at The Lowell.

The Lowell lobby was quiet in a practiced way. The carpet softened every footstep. A man behind the desk nodded once when she entered, the kind of acknowledgment that suggested he already knew she belonged.

The elevator rose without a sound. Belle watched the numbers change and resisted the urge to check her reflection in the mirrored panel. Celeste had warned her: elevators were where people revealed nervousness.

The man was older—late fifties, silver hair, careful hands. He wore wealth lightly, as if it were an old coat.

“You’re new,” he said.

She waited two beats.

"Yes."

"I was told you are observant."

Another beat.

"Observation without accuracy is just watching," she said.

He smiled, faintly.

Dinner arrived on a wheeled cart.

A waiter in a dark jacket entered quietly behind it. Silver covers lifted from the plates with a soft metallic sound. Linen unfolded across the small table near the window. The bottle was presented, opened, poured.

He moved with careful neutrality, eyes lowered just enough to avoid involvement.

When he left, the door closed without a sound.

The gentleman did not reach for her immediately.

He spoke about shipping contracts and a foundation board in Connecticut.

She listened. Asked measured questions.

Let silence sit long enough to matter.

When his hand finally touched her wrist, she rotated it subtly, guiding pressure instead of resisting.

He noticed.

"Confident," he murmured.

"Composed," she corrected gently.

❧

After the appointment, the city felt louder.

She walked two blocks before sitting on a bench near Lexington.

The avenue moved faster than the side streets. Buses sighed at the curb and taxis pressed forward between delivery trucks as if the city had decided patience was inefficient. The wind cut between buildings and struck her collarbones.

Across the street a Korean deli blazed with fluorescent light, its awning crowded with buckets of flowers—dahlias, sunflowers, roses in cellophane—incongruously bright against the darkening avenue. Belle noticed that a leaf had fallen onto her coat and brushed it aside. A man in a delivery uniform emerged carrying two brown bags, already moving before the door had closed b ehind him. A woman in a long coat chose a bunch of white roses without stopping, handing bills to the man behind the register in a single practiced motion.

Belle watched her walk away, roses against her coat, already gone. In Mississippi you bought flowers for funerals and graduations. Here they were sold at ten p.m. on a Tuesday to women who were already somewhere else in their minds.

She sat until her pulse steadied.

Then she stood and walked north.

She had performed adequately.

She had not disappeared.

That was enough.

Chapter 17

The man Celeste sent her to that Thursday was named Aldrich.

No first name offered. No explanation of what he did or had done or continued to do that allowed him to live the way he lived. Celeste's notes said only: *old family, foundation work, prefers conversation, dislikes effort.*

Belle understood the last part immediately.

He was waiting when she arrived—not at the bar, not checking his phone, simply seated in the armchair nearest the window with the particular stillness of a man who had stopped needing to perform patience because he had actually acquired it. Seventy perhaps. White hair cut short. A suit that had been made for him sometime in the previous decade and still fit because he had not changed. No watch visible. No signals.

He stood when she entered.

"Miss Devereaux," he said.

"Mr. Aldrich."

He gestured toward the table near the window. Dinner was already arranged—not ordered, arranged. Someone had done this before she arrived. The wine was open and breathing. The lighting had been adjusted. Small things, done quietly, that said: I have been here before, and I know how this works and I wanted it to be correct.

Belle sat.

She picked up the menu without opening it.

"You won't need that," Aldrich said. "I took the liberty."

"Of course," Belle said.

The way you acknowledge something that has already happened and does not require your opinion.

Aldrich looked at her for a moment with the unhurried attention of someone who had been reading people for fifty years and was no longer in any hurry about it.

Then he picked up his wine.

"Tell me something that isn't on any page," he said.

Belle let the silence sit for exactly the right length of time.

"The violin in a Braque painting," she said, "doesn't have to look like a violin. It only has to participate in a conversation powerful enough to endure."

Aldrich's hand paused almost imperceptibly on his glass.

"You've been to the Art Institute," he said.

"Chicago," Belle said. "Some time ago."

"What else did you see?"

"A football player made of rectangles," she said. "A horizon that refused to lie flat."

Aldrich smiled. Not the smile of a man being charmed. The smile of a man who has stopped expecting something and received it anyway.

"Malevich," he said.

"The placard said so," Belle replied.

He laughed then—a genuine sound, unguarded, the laugh of someone who has forgotten for a moment to be composed.

Belle noted the exact moment it happened.

Not with satisfaction. With something quieter than that.

❧

They talked for two hours.

Not about markets or about foundation boards or acquisitions or the peculiar psychology of men who needed to win small arguments. They talked about cities and what cities did to people over time. About the particular loneliness of rooms that had been designed for discretion. About a painter Aldrich had known in the seventies who had refused to sell a single work until he was sixty and by then the market had moved past him entirely.

"He didn't care," Aldrich said.

"Did that make it better or worse?" Belle asked.

Aldrich considered that for a long moment.

"Better," he said finally. "And worse."

Belle turned her glass slowly.

"Both at once," she said.

"Yes," Aldrich said. "That's usually how it works."

He looked at her across the table with the same unhurried attention he had brought to everything all evening.

"You're not what I expected," he said.

Belle waited.

"Celeste sends me capable women," he continued. "Accomplished. Precise." He paused. "You're present."

"There's a difference," Belle said.

"Yes," he said. "There is."

He did not elaborate.

He didn't need to.

Afterward Belle walked south on Madison.

The avenue moved with its usual polished indifference. Black cars. Store windows. The cold coming off the cross streets in clean pulses.

She walked two blocks before she understood what had shifted.

The persona had not felt like a persona tonight.

It had felt like arriving somewhere she had been moving toward for a long time without knowing the address. It had not felt like performance or translation, not like the careful architecture of a woman assembling herself before entering a room.

It had felt like arrival.

Just—herself. Wearing well.

Belle Devereaux was not simply a name Celeste had given her.

It was a name she had grown into.

She stopped at the corner of Sixty-Eighth and looked up at the buildings running south along the avenue, their windows lit against the dark, each one containing something private and specific that the street would never know.

She understood something then that she had not understood before.

Whatever came next—and something always came next—it would be threatening to take this.

The thing she had just discovered she actually was.

She stood at the corner of Sixty-Eighth for a moment without moving.

The avenue ran south in both directions, its windows lit, its traffic steady and indifferent. A doorman across the street stepped outside briefly, looked at the sky, and stepped back in. A woman walked past with a small dog that was having opinions about the cold. Two men in dark coats moved through the intersection without looking at each other or at Belle or at anything except the middle distance where their next obligation waited.

Nobody knew what had just happened in that room.

Nobody knew that a woman had spent two hours being genuinely present with another person for the first time in longer than she could accurately measure. That she had talked about Braque and Malevich and a painter who refused to sell his work and the peculiar loneliness of rooms designed for discretion. That a man of seventy had laughed—actually laughed, unguarded and unperformed—because she had said something true.

Nobody knew.

The city didn't require them to.

Belle touched the inside of her wrist. The moth was warm beneath her thumb the way it sometimes was, in the way skin holds heat when something has moved through it.

She had not noticed until now.

She breathed in once.

Cold air. Car exhaust. The faint ghost of someone's coffee from a cart that had closed an hour ago.

New York.

Hers.

She turned up her collar.

And walked back into the city that had made her.

Chapter 18

It was Angelique who broke the distance.

She simply appeared in the kitchen doorway one evening holding a bottle of wine that cost less than the glasses they usually used and said, "I hate drinking alone," as if that settled it.

They sat at the kitchen table without ceremony. Shoes off. Makeup removed. The apartment less composed, more human. Outside, the city moved through another ordinary night.

Angelique poured without asking how much.

"How are you finding it?" she asked.

Belle considered the question carefully, the way Celeste had taught her.

Angelique noticed.

"You don't have to do that here," she said.

Belle looked at her.

"Do what?"

"Count to two before you answer." Angelique's mouth curved slightly. "I'm not a client."

Belle felt something loosen in her chest that she hadn't realized was tight.

"Strange," she said finally. "I'm finding it strange."

"Good," Angelique said. "Strange means you're paying attention."

She sipped her wine.

"It gets less strange," she added. "That's not entirely a good thing."

Belle turned her glass slowly.

"Does it bother you?" she asked. "The work?"

Angelique considered that with the same honesty she seemed to bring to everything.

"Sometimes," she said. "Less than it used to."

"Why less?"

"Because I stopped waiting for it to feel like something it isn't." She set her glass down. "It's work. Work has rules. Follow the rules and most nights you go home intact."

Belle waited.

"Most nights," she repeated.

Angelique met her eyes.

"Most nights," she confirmed.

The wine sat between them.

"Never drink from a client's glass," Angelique said after a moment, not as instruction but the way you pass someone a piece of information you wish someone had passed you. "Ever."

"Okay."

"Always carry cash. Enough to leave from anywhere. Not a card. Cash."

Belle nodded.

"And if something tightens here—" Angelique pressed two fingers briefly to her sternum "—you go. You don't finish the evening. You don't calculate the fee. You go."

"Celeste—"

"Celeste calculates," Angelique said quietly. "Calculation has margins." She looked at her glass. "Your gut doesn't."

The statement arrived without drama.

Only experience.

Belle watched her for a moment.

"Has your gut ever been wrong?" she asked.

Angelique almost smiled.

"Yes," she said. "But I was always glad I listened to it anyway."

They stayed at the table another hour.

They talked about other things after that—a restaurant on Lexington Angelique liked, a client who had once arrived with his college roommate without warning, a coat she had seen in a window on Madison that she couldn't justify and couldn't stop thinking about.

Small things.

Ordinary things.

The kind of things people talk about when they are simply in a room together and neither of them wants to leave yet.

When Angelique finally stood and said goodnight, her steps down the hallway were less measured than usual.

Belle sat alone at the table for a while longer.

The bond between them was not yet warmth.

But it was the beginning of something real.

And in this city, in this life, that was not nothing.

Chapter 19

The kitchen window was open an inch despite the cold.

Leila sat on the counter filing her nails. Mei stood at the stove warming tea she had no intention of drinking. Sofia leaned back in a chair with her legs crossed, scrolling lazily through her phone.

Belle had been listening for several minutes before she spoke.

"Who is Daniel Pierce?"

Sofia laughed first.

"Oh, that one."

Leila glanced up.

"Celeste finally sending him someone new?"

"No," Belle said.

"Then don't ask," Leila replied. "You'll make it happen."

Mei poured the tea and set the kettle aside.

"He pays a retainer," she said.

Belle looked up.

"For what?"

"Access," Sofia said. "Whenever he wants."

Leila shrugged.

"He likes control."

Sofia shook her head.

"No. He likes watching people try to keep control."

Belle waited.

Leila slipped off the counter.

"The first time I met him he changed the restaurant twice while I was already in the car."

"Why?" Belle asked.

Leila smiled faintly.

"To see if I would complain."

"Did you?"

"No."

"Why not?"

Leila looked at her.

"Because Celeste told me not to."

Sofia set her phone down.

"He once asked me what I would do if he cancelled an appointment after I arrived."

"What did you say?" Belle asked.

"I told him I would go shopping."

Leila laughed.

"And?"

"He didn't cancel," Sofia said. "But he looked disappointed."

Mei leaned against the counter.

"He moves things," she said quietly.

Belle turned to her.

"What do you mean?"

"Time. Locations. Conversation." Mei's voice remained calm. "He shifts something small and watches what happens."

Angelique entered the kitchen just then, carrying a glass of water.

"What are we talking about?"

"Pierce," Sofia said.

Angelique paused.

"That man again."

Belle watched her.

"You've met him?"

Angelique nodded once.

"What was he like?" Belle asked.

Angelique considered the question carefully.

"Polite," she said.

"That doesn't sound dangerous," Sofia replied.

Angelique looked at Belle instead.

"The dangerous ones never do."

Leila slipped her shoes back on.

"Well," she said lightly, "if Celeste sends him Belle, we'll see how patient he really is."

Mei met Belle's eyes.

"He remembers everything."

Angelique added the last piece.

"And he never runs the same test twice."

Chapter 20

Betsy had decided this one was different.

He wore boots that cost more than his truck. Polished. Heavy leather that did not bend easily. He called her darlin' in public and girl in private. He paid for groceries twice, even when she insisted she had it covered.

"I told him not to fix that hallway wall," Betsy said. "Now the paint don't match."

Annabelle paused. "What was wrong with the wall?"

"Nothing," Betsy said too quickly. "Door swung open too hard. Old hinges. You know how these old trailers are."

In the background, a cabinet closed.

"He just likes things neat," Betsy added. "Billy don't like a mess."

Annabelle stood in her kitchen with granite countertops, the counters cold beneath her palm, a thousand miles and several economies away.

"Are you safe?" she asked.

Betsy laughed.

"You always ask that like I ain't grown."

In the background, a male voice:

“Who you talkin’ to?”

It wasn't loud or slurred, but definitely at home.

“Annabelle,” Betsy called back.

A pause.

Long enough to register.

Then the voice again, closer now. “Tell her hello.”

“Billy says hello,” Betsy said, brightness returning on cue.

Belle pictured the hallway. The patch drying lighter than the rest of the wall. A square of paint that hadn’t settled yet.

“Does he get angry?” she asked.

“Everybody gets angry,” Betsy said. “He works hard.”

Another pause.

“He just don’t like disrespect.”

The word settled.

From the modern kitchen, structure looked elegant. Contained. Negotiated.

In Yazoo City, structure wore boots and fixed steps and called it protection.

Belle said nothing more.

She had learned that silence unsettled men.

She was not sure yet what it did to women.

Chapter 21

Celeste did not send Belle back to the same kind of man twice in a row.

Variety was not a courtesy.

It was training.

This appointment was not a dinner.

It was an afternoon.

The Mark lobby was brighter than The Lowell had been, its furniture arranged in sharp white lines. Two women in black coats crossed the floor speaking French as if they owned the afternoon.

The elevator walls were mirrored. A woman in black stood beside her scrolling through a phone that cost more than Belle's first car. Neither of them spoke.

The suite at The Mark had its curtains half-drawn, daylight filtered into gold. The room smelled faintly of citrus polish and someone else's cologne—expensive, restrained.

He was younger than the first.

Mid-thirties. Good hair. A watch that was too deliberate. He carried his body like a man who had discovered money recently and still expected it to perform for him.

He looked Belle up and down in a single smooth motion and smiled as if he believed that was charm.

"Celeste says you're smart," he said.

Belle waited.

"Celeste says a lot of things," she replied.

His smile widened. "That's what I mean. You're... quick."

He poured drinks without asking if she wanted one.

Angelique's Rule One surfaced in Belle's mind like a reflex.

The man lifted his glass. "To new arrangements."

Belle's hands remained still. "I don't drink at work."

He laughed softly. "Oh, come on. It's not a job-job."

Belle watched him for one full beat.

"It is," she said.

The words landed cleanly. The room shifted slightly. Not hostile—recalibrated.

He set his drink down and studied her. "You're very restrained."

Belle let the silence do its work.

"This upholstery is lovely," she said after several seconds.

A flicker of irritation crossed his face before he replaced it with amusement.

"Okay," he said, as if conceding a point he had not earned the right to debate. "Conversation first. That's fine."

He wanted to talk about power. That was clear within minutes. Not in policy terms. In terms of access.

He spoke about a partner who had been "too public" with a scandal. About women who "didn't understand discretion." About how quickly reputations collapsed when people lacked discipline.

Belle listened with the faintest edge of interest.

He was telling her who he was without realizing it: a man who feared embarrassment more than consequence.

At one point he leaned forward slightly and lowered his voice.

"What does Celeste have you doing?" he asked. "Like... what's the real arrangement?"

There it was.

Not curiosity.

Boundary pressure disguised as intimacy.

Belle felt the old reflex again—to deflect with a joke, to soften, to make herself likable so he would not turn unpredictable.

Mississippi reflex.

She recognized it now the way you recognized a bad road you had driven too fast before.

Belle kept her face neutral.

"Celeste has me doing exactly what you paid for," she said.

He laughed, but it was less comfortable this time. "I like you."

"I'm pleasant," Belle replied. "Liking is not required."

The man sat back. He watched her with a new kind of attention—not appraisal, not hunger.

Calculation.

Belle understood then what Celeste had been teaching her.

It wasn't how to be pretty.

It was how to survive men who believed purchase included permission.

The man reached for her wrist lightly, testing.

Belle rotated her hand the way she had learned—not pulling away, not resisting. Redirecting pressure. Controlling contact without creating a scene.

His fingers loosened.

He blinked, surprised.

"Interesting," he murmured, and for the first time he sounded unsure.

Belle held his gaze.

"If you want something different," she said, quiet but precise, "you say it. And I decide."

There was a pause—the kind where men decide whether they are being challenged or instructed.

He exhaled once. "Fair."

The rest of the hour passed without incident.

When the appointment ended, he walked her to the door like a man performing manners for himself.

In the elevator, Belle stared at the numbers descending and felt her heart begin to thud harder.

Not fear.

Aftershock.

She stepped onto the sidewalk and turned south on Madison.

Madison in December was its own argument. The buildings here did not lean toward the street the way buildings did in other parts of the city. They stood back slightly, as if the avenue itself required room to be looked at. The shops did not advertise loudly. They did not need to. Their clientele already knew they were there and everyone else was not the point.

A woman emerged from a building two doors down, a small bag hanging from one wrist, and stood on the sidewalk for a moment adjusting her gloves. Her coat was camel. Her shoes were low and exact. She looked neither left nor right before stepping into a waiting car.

Belle watched her go.

She thought about the Art Institute. About the paintings held in place by agreement. About how the woman's coat was not beautiful exactly—it was correct. Correct for this street, this season, this particular arrangement of money and restraint.

She had been learning the language.

Standing on Madison Avenue in December, she understood for the first time that she was becoming fluent.

The avenue moved with polished indifference. Black cars idled at the curb. Store windows had begun to change—dark glass replaced by small forests of silver ornaments and white lights arranged with deliberate restraint. A doorman across the street stood beside a doorway framed in evergreen garland, its scent faint even from the sidewalk.

The wind came sharp between buildings, slicing through the seams of her coat.

She walked two blocks before stopping near a bench and sitting.

A man pushed a cart stacked with wreaths past the corner florist. The bells tied to the cart handles chimed softly as he turned.

A taxi rushed past, horn sharp in the air.

Her hands trembled faintly—not from cold but from the realization that the moment had mattered.

She had not been brave.

She had been prepared.

❧

Back at the apartment, Angelique stood in the kitchen with a mug of tea, watching Belle remove her coat slowly, deliberately, the way Celeste had insisted.

Angelique's gaze flicked once to Belle's hands.

"You okay?" she asked.

Belle nodded. "Yes."

Angelique waited, as if she understood that yes could mean many things.

"He tried to change the terms," Belle added.

Angelique's jaw tightened almost imperceptibly. "And?"

"I didn't let him."

Angelique studied her for a beat longer, then nodded once.

"Good," she said.

It wasn't praise.

It was confirmation that Belle was still alive in the correct way.

That night, Belle lay in bed and listened to the city move beneath the windows.

Somewhere, far below, someone shouted. A siren rose and fell. A truck backed into an alley with three short beeps like punctuation.

Belle did not close her eyes immediately.

She replayed the moment in the suite—the question, the pressure, the quiet refusal.

Then she let it go.

That was new too.

Chapter 22

The first time all four of them were in a room together, it was not planned.

Afterward, they found each other in the lobby the way women sometimes find each other after difficult evenings—not by arrangement, simply by the pull of recognizing someone who understood without explanation.

Leila arrived first. She was already at the bar with a glass of sparkling water when Belle came through the door, and she raised it slightly in acknowledgment the way you raise a glass to someone you have not yet decided about.

Mei appeared five minutes later. She took the stool beside Leila without asking, ordered nothing, and sat watching the room with the particular patience of someone who had decided the room was more interesting than anything she might say about it.

Belle sat.

For a moment nobody spoke.

The lobby bar at The Mark was quieter than the floors above it, the piano the only thing that suggested the evening was still in progress. A pianist played something European and forgettable in the corner. Two men at a table near the window were performing a negotiation in lowered voices, their body language the particular choreography of men who wanted to appear casual and were not.

Mei looked at them briefly.

"The one on the left will get what he wants," she said.

Leila glanced over.

"Why."

"He's been still for twenty minutes. The other one keeps adjusting."

Belle looked.

The man on the left had his hands flat on the table. The man on the right had moved his phone twice, his water glass once, and was now straightening a cocktail napkin that did not need straightening.

Leila nodded slowly.

"How long have you been doing that?" Belle asked Mei.

Mei considered the question.

"Reading rooms?"

"Yes."

"Since I was eight," she said. "My mother ran a restaurant. You learn quickly which tables are going to be trouble."

Leila set her glass down.

"My father sold cars," she said. "Same principle."

Belle thought of Phil's Fill-R-Ups. Of Dewey Ray counting cigarettes before dawn. Of the men who came in at two in the morning and the particular quality of attention you developed when you needed to know within thirty seconds whether someone was going to be a problem.

She didn't say any of that.

But something in her posture must have changed because Leila looked at her with the sharp, assessing eyes she brought to everything.

"Truck stop," Leila said.

Not a question.

Belle met her gaze.

"Gas station."

Leila almost smiled.

"Same education," she said.

Angelique arrived then, sliding onto the last stool with the ease of someone who had been late to things her entire life and had long ago made peace with it.

"Sorry," she said, not sounding it. "His driver was slow."

She looked at the three of them arranged along the bar.

"Did I miss anything?"

"Origin stories," Leila said.

Angelique raised an eyebrow.

"Mine is boring," she said.

"They always are," Mei replied.

The pianist moved to something else. The two men at the table reached a conclusion, the one on the right finally going still. Belle watched him accept whatever he had just agreed to with the composed expression of someone who had known twenty minutes ago how it was going to end.

She filed that away.

They sat for another half hour, talking about small things—a restaurant on Ninth that Angelique liked, a client Leila had rescheduled twice without explanation, the particular tedium of men who believed their taste in wine was a personality. Nobody talked about the work directly. Nobody needed to.

When they left they went separately, the way they always did.

But something had been established.

Not friendship exactly.

Something more durable than that.

Recognition.

Chapter 23

It was Leila's idea.

She arrived at the apartment on a Wednesday with a deck of cards and a bottle of something cheap and red that she set on the kitchen table without apology.

"Hearts," she said. "Four players. I'm tired of thinking."

Angelique looked at the bottle.

"That's not wine," she said.

"No," Leila agreed. "It isn't."

Mei arrived twenty minutes later with nothing, which was correct—she had been called, she had come, that was her contribution. She sat at the table and looked at the deck with the expression of someone who had already assessed the situation and found it acceptable.

Belle found four glasses that didn't match and set them out.

Nobody commented on that either.

❧

Leila dealt with the particular efficiency of someone who had been dealing cards since childhood—not showy, just fast, the deck moving through her hands like she had never needed to think about it.

"Do you know Hearts?" she asked Belle.

"I know the rules."

"Knowing the rules and playing Hearts are different things," Leila said.

"How."

Angelique picked up her hand and arranged it without looking up.

"Hearts is about what you're willing to give away," she said.

Leila smiled.

"And what you're willing to get caught holding."

❧

The first hand was quiet.

The second not so much. They passed cards without ceremony—each woman sending her most dangerous cards to the right, receiving three unknowns from the left, recalculating. Belle looked at what she'd been passed and understood immediately that Angelique had given her nothing useful and kept everything she needed.

She filed that.

The play moved around the table. Leila took the first trick, then gave it up gracefully on the second. Angelique played with a kind of relaxed precision that suggested she already knew how the hand would end and was simply moving through it at the appropriate pace.

Mei played nothing that revealed anything.

By the third trick Belle was watching her.

Not her cards. Her hands. The specific stillness of them between plays. The way she set each card down without hesitation, without the small tell of someone deciding at the last moment.

Mei was not deciding.

She had already decided.

❧

By the fourth trick, Belle was certain.

"She's going for it," she said quietly.

Leila looked up.

"Already?"

"Look at what she's not taking."

Leila studied the table. Then she looked at Mei with the sharp appraising eyes she brought to everything.

Mei did not look up from her cards.

"The hand is what it is," she said.

"We can stop you," Leila said.

"You can try," Mei replied.

It was the most words she had spoken all evening.

❧

They tried.

Leila led a club she didn't want to lead, trying to draw out Mei's high cards early. Angelique played a careful diamond that said nothing and meant everything—a signal to Belle, whose turn came next, that she should do the same.

Belle understood.

She played accordingly.

Mei absorbed it all.

She took the trick. And the next. And the next. Each card falling from her hand with the same quiet inevitability, the same absence of drama, as if the outcome had been decided somewhere before the game began and the four of them were simply moving through the confirmation of it.

Nobody had led spades yet. They had all been avoiding it the way you avoid a conversation you know is coming.

The Bitch came out on the seventh trick.

Leila whispered, "Celeste," with a giggle.

Mei took it without expression.

Leila set her remaining cards face down on the table.

"I have nothing that helps," she said.

Angelique looked at her hand.

"Neither do I."

Belle held three hearts and a decision.

She looked at Mei.

Mei met her eyes for the first time since the hand began. There was nothing in her expression that asked for anything. No appeal. No performance of confidence. Just the particular stillness of a woman who had assessed the situation completely and was waiting for the world to catch up.

Belle played her lowest heart.

Mei took it.

Then the next two tricks in succession, clean and unhurried, the cards accumulating in front of her like something that had always been heading her way.

When it was over Mei set her hand face down on the table.

Twenty-six points distributed equally to the other three.

Leila poured herself more wine that wasn't wine.

"I knew from the first trick," she said. "I saw it, and I still couldn't stop it."

"Nobody could stop it," Angelique said. "That's the point."

Belle looked at Mei.

"How did you know you had it?"

Mei considered that for a moment.

"I didn't know," she said. "I knew the hand was strong enough to try. The difference between trying and succeeding is what the other players do."

"We tried to stop you," Belle said.

"Yes," Mei said. "And you did everything correctly." She picked up her glass. "The hand was just stronger."

Leila looked at the ceiling.

"That's deeply unfair," she said.

"Yes," Mei agreed pleasantly.

❧

They played two more hands.

Neither was as interesting as the second.

The wine that wasn't wine ran out somewhere in the third hand and Angelique produced a bottle of something better from the back of a cabinet without explaining where it had come from, and nobody asked.

Outside the apartment window Manhattan moved through another ordinary night—sirens, taxis, the distant percussion of the city doing what the city did. Inside, the table held four women and a deck of cards and the particular warmth of a room where the armor had been set down somewhere between the first deal and the last trick and nobody had bothered to pick it back up.

At some point Leila said, not to anyone in particular:

"We should do this again."

Nobody disagreed.

Mei gathered the cards and squared the deck with the same precise attention she brought to everything.

She set it in the center of the table.

Left it there for whoever needed it next.

Chapter 24

After a few months, Belle stopped noticing the corrections as corrections.

They arrived the way the weather arrived in New York—not dramatic, just constant pressure until you adjusted your posture without thinking.

Celeste's calendar did not read like a schedule. It read like a system.

Tuesday: dinner with a man who collected contemporary sculpture and spoke in polished blocks of thought.

Thursday: cocktails with a hedge fund partner who asked too many questions about her childhood as if poverty were a fetish.

Saturday: a private room at a restaurant where the staff did not make eye contact, which was part of the service.

Belle learned that wealth did not share a single personality.

It shared habits.

They all arrived on time. They all expected silence to be used correctly. They all watched the room the way hunters watched a tree line—not frantic, simply attentive to advantage.

The hotel names began to blur: Lowell, Mark, Carlyle, Baccarat. Places that smelled like clean linen and money that had never been handled by the people who spent it.

The elevator door had to close before she checked her reflection in its steel.

The phone belonged in her hand as if it hardly mattered.

A concierge required exactly the right amount of acknowledgment—not warmth, not dismissal. Neutrality with a spine.

“It would be nicer,” he said, “if you stayed longer. Just another hour. I’ll make it worth it.”

Belle did not answer immediately.

Celeste’s training lived in her throat now like a held note.

“No,” Belle said evenly.

The man smiled as if he admired her. “I didn’t mean to offend.”

“I wasn’t offended,” she replied.

Two beats.

“I’m simply not available.”

The man watched her for a second longer than comfort.

Then he nodded.

The check arrived on schedule. The envelope was thick. The exit was clean.

Celeste met her afterward in the car. She did not congratulate her. Celeste rarely congratulated.

“You didn’t fill space,” Celeste said. “Good.”

Belle stared out the window as the city slid past, glass towers repeating like teeth.

“How many times before it feels normal?” she asked.

Celeste’s mouth tilted slightly. Not amusement. Recognition.

“It never feels normal,” Celeste said. “It feels governed.”

The vocabulary mattered.

Governed meant contained by rule, not soothed by familiarity. Belle understood that immediately.

At home, Angelique moved through the apartment as if it were a hotel suite she did not intend to personalize. Shoes aligned. Makeup closed. Nothing left open long enough to suggest vulnerability.

But sometimes, late at night, Angelique would stand in the kitchen in a thin robe and drink water with both hands wrapped around the glass as if she were cold.

"You're doing fine," Angelique said once, not looking at Belle.

Belle paused. "That's not praise."

Angelique gave her a glance that was almost a smile. "No. It's information."

Outside, the air changed.

The first time Belle noticed it, it was on Fifth Avenue along the park—a thin sharpness that cut through her coat and made her step faster before she remembered not to.

Celeste saw it.

"Slow down," she said. "Cold makes people reveal themselves."

Belle adjusted her pace. Her breath became a quiet discipline.

It was March and the Christmas decorations were long gone. The avenue felt different without them—longer somehow, more itself, the limestone facades returning to their natural neutrality after weeks of performed warmth.

New York in March did not apologize for what it was.

Snow had come twice already, the first time overnight so that Belle woke to a city she didn't recognize—the same grid, the same buildings, but softened, every hard edge rounded, the usual noise replaced by something that wasn't quite silence but was the closest the city ever came to it. She had stood at the apartment window in the early morning dark and watched a single cab move through the unplowed street below, its tires leaving clean tracks that filled again almost immediately.

By noon it was gone. The city had absorbed it the way the city absorbed everything—efficiently, without sentiment, moving forward before the snow had finished melting.

The second time it came during the day. She was walking on Fifth when it started—small flakes at first, almost imperceptible, then thicker, the park across the street going pale and soft behind a gauze of white. People around her did not stop. They adjusted—collars up, pace slightly quickened, phones put away—and continued. The city accommodating the weather without conceding to it.

Belle kept walking.

She had learned that from the city itself.

Across the avenue, Central Park stood stripped of leaves, the trees black against the winter sky. The wind moved cleanly through the branches and out into the street.

The city did not soften.

It had simply changed texture.

Time moved in accumulations.

❧

One evening, Belle stood at the mirror in the hallway and realized her face had changed without her permission.

Not prettier.

More decided.

Less pleading.

She did not know exactly when it had happened.

Only that it had.

When Celeste mentioned Daniel Pierce, Belle did not feel flattered.

"Some clients purchase evenings," Celeste said. "Pierce purchases influence."

She had heard his name from other girls.

They spoke it carefully.

She didn't know who he was exactly—only that she had heard his name, and he was important.

Chapter 25

The taxi dropped them at the corner of Prince and Mercer, the engine's rattle swallowed by the deeper, more ancient hum of SoHo at night. Behind them, the luxury boutiques—the glass-fronted cathedrals of Dior and Chanel—stood like dark, silent monuments to the visibility they had spent all evening performing.

"Inside," Leila said, her voice dropping the melodic, neutral tone she used for clients. She didn't wait for Belle to agree.

Fanelli's Cafe didn't have a velvet rope. It had a heavy wooden door that had been swinging open since the mid-1800s, and when they stepped through, the air hit Belle like a physical weight. It didn't smell like the expensive, filtered citrus of Celeste's townhouse or the sterile luxury of The Mark. It smelled of spilled beer, frying onions, and a century of floor wax.

The lighting was a warm, unapologetic yellow that didn't do anyone any favors. There were no "clean lines" or "diffused light" here—only the cluttered geometry of a place that had refused to change for anyone.

They found a booth in the back, the red vinyl cracked and taped at the edges. Leila didn't sit; she collapsed, kicking her Louboutins off under the table with a dull thud that sounded like a surrender.

"My god," Leila muttered, rubbing her arches. "If I have to talk about revenue variance for one more hour, I'm going to walk into the Hudson".

A waitress appeared, wearing a t-shirt for a local band and an expression that said she wouldn't recognize a "Belle Devereaux" if she were wearing a crown. She set plastic-wrapped menus on the table without a word.

"Burgers," Angelique said, her eyes fixed on the neon Budweiser sign humming over the bar. "And the cheapest fries they have. No truffle oil. No reduction. Just salt."

Belle watched the room. At the bar, a group of construction workers in dusty boots sat next to a man in a rumpled suit reading a paperback. No one was measuring the "symmetry" of her face. No one was "assessing the structure" of her bones. For the first time since she'd left Mississippi, Belle felt the exhilarating relief of being absolutely, professionally invisible.

"Celeste would have a stroke if she saw the health code rating on that wall," Belle said, the ghost of a smile touching her mouth.

"Celeste isn't here," Mei said, sliding a thick glass of water toward her. It wasn't served from a crystal pitcher, and it didn't taste "cold enough to hurt". It was just water. "In this room, we aren't 'assets.' We're just hungry".

They sat in the low, steady noise of the cafe—a shared silence that wasn't a "measuring stick" or a "rehearsal," but a safe harbor. Outside, the "machine" of the city continued its brutal, indifferent rhythm, but inside the cracked vinyl booth at Fanelli's, the architecture was finally down, and they were just four women owning their territory quietly.

Chapter 26

Celeste had chosen Café Boulud.

The maître d' greeted Pierce with the calm familiarity reserved for men who did not need reservations.

The dining room was quiet in the expensive way quiet places are—voices low, tables spaced far enough apart that conversations dissolved before reaching the next one. Waiters moved with careful economy, as if unnecessary motion had been priced out of the room.

Daniel Pierce stood when they arrived.

He was older than Belle expected. Late fifties perhaps. His hands were controlled, the movements small and exact. A wedding ring caught the light briefly when he reached for Celeste's chair.

"Celeste."

"Daniel."

The greeting carried familiarity without warmth.

His attention moved to Belle.

Assessing.

"Belle," Celeste said.

Pierce inclined his head slightly, acknowledging the name the way a collector acknowledges provenance.

They sat.

The waiter poured wine without asking who should be served first.

Pierce.

Then Celeste.

Then Belle.

Celeste conducted the conversation.

Art acquisitions. A museum board in Boston. A vineyard Pierce had purchased in Napa because, he explained, "land is easier to improve than people."

Pierce spoke with the relaxed certainty of a man accustomed to decisions being implemented after he expressed them.

Celeste never contradicted him.

But she did not defer either.

Belle listened.

She noticed how the waiter returned to Pierce first whenever the glasses needed refilling. How the couple at the next table lowered their voices slightly after recognizing him.

Power moved through Manhattan quietly.

When Pierce addressed her, it arrived without warning.

"And what do you think?"

The question was light. The room remained calm.

Belle waited two beats.

"I think most people confuse visibility with importance."

Celeste did not look at her.

Pierce did.

He set his fork down.

"And you don't?"

"I try not to."

A small pause settled over the table.

Celeste lifted her glass.

"Belle has been learning the difference between being noticed and being necessary."

Pierce regarded her again, longer this time.

The conversation resumed.

Wine. Weather in Napa. A foundation dinner in May.

But Belle felt the shift.

After dinner, Celeste said nothing until they were in the car.

"You did not rush," she said finally. "You did not fill space."

Belle watched the lights move along Madison Avenue.

"Will he come back?"

Celeste's expression did not change.

"He already has."

Across the street, a man in a gray coat photographed the license plate.

Chapter 27

Betsy called at an hour she never used to call.

Belle answered on the second ring.

"Are you okay?" she asked immediately.

"Why wouldn't I be?" Betsy replied, too quickly.

There was a pause. A television in the background. A door closing somewhere out of range.

"How's Billy?" Belle asked.

"Oh, he's fine. Works hard. You know."

No elaboration.

"I sent some money," Belle said.

"You don't have to—"

"I know."

Another pause.

"You sound different," Betsy said.

"I am."

That silence lengthened.

"New York change you already?" Betsy asked, not unkindly.

"It teaches you," Belle said.

"Teach you what?"

"That nothing holds unless you hold it."

Betsy laughed lightly. It did not land.

"He's been stressed," Betsy added. "That's all."

The word settled.

Stressed.

Belle leaned against the kitchen counter.

"Are you safe?" she asked.

"I ain't a child."

No answer.

After hanging up, Belle remained standing there.

Angelique emerged from her room but did not approach.

"Mississippi?" she asked.

"Yes."

Angelique nodded once.

"They don't leave us," she said.

Belle did not respond.

Later, she wired more money than necessary.

Money did not repair what mattered.

It purchased time.

That night, she stood at the apartment window and watched Manhattan flicker below. The city lights blinked without sentiment. Cars moved like deliberate signals across an illuminated grid.

She tried to determine whether she was running toward something structured—or simply running faster than something unstructured could follow.

She did not yet know.

But she closed the blinds.

Chapter 28

Belle learned quickly that the rules were rarely spoken.

Celeste never issued a handbook. There was no list taped to a mirror, no formal contract explaining the choreography of rooms where money and desire intersected. Instead, the rules lived in the pauses between instructions.

They were enforced socially.

The first rule Belle noticed was **time**.

Clients did not arrive late. If they did, it meant something—either arrogance or testing. Neither was accidental.

The second rule was **attention**.

Men of a certain level did not want flattery. They wanted recognition. Not of their money—that was assumed—but of their position in the invisible architecture of power. Belle learned to watch the signals: how a man greeted a waiter, whether he checked his phone face-up or face-down, how he spoke about people who were not in the room.

Desire, she realized, was rarely the primary transaction.

Control was.

Belle did not flirt in the way girls at Phil's Fill-R-Ups had flirted with truck drivers. She listened. She let silence expand until men filled it with confessions disguised as opinions.

"You're very calm," one banker observed over dinner at The Lowell.

Belle held his gaze for a moment longer than politeness required.

"I prefer accurate," she said.

He laughed as if she had told a joke.

But he did not interrupt her again.

By the end of July, she understood something that had never existed in Mississippi: men who were powerful enough did not need to shout.

They expected the world to arrange itself around them.

And increasingly, Belle found that it did.

Outside, New York was doing what New York did with summer—absorbing it without conceding to it. The heat came off the pavement in waves and collected in the cross streets and the city moved through it exactly as it moved through everything else, without adjustment, without complaint. Mississippi summer had weight and smell and intention. This was different. This was just heat with nowhere to go.

She was learning to move through both kinds.

Chapter 29

She stopped keeping track of names.

Details blurred: the shape of a watch face, the scent of a particular cologne, the way a man's voice pitched at the end of a question. She learned to catalog only what mattered—exits, windows, the mood in a room five minutes before trouble showed itself.

Sometimes there was no trouble. Sometimes the evening was a transaction, clean and dull, and she left with her mind pleasantly empty.

But at times, something was off. A question that lingered too long. A hand that hovered a fraction too close. A story that drifted, unfinished, into silence.

Belle learned to manage silence. To wait longer than the other person. To let discomfort fill the space, then shape it to her advantage.

She noticed patterns. Clients who wanted to be guided. Others who needed to be disarmed. Some who mistook her stillness for shyness, and some who found it unnerving.

She began to sense, with a kind of animal intuition, when a night would turn. Sometimes she could steer it back; sometimes she simply endured, clocking the minutes until the car arrived.

Celeste never asked for details. She looked at the numbers, the reviews, the referrals. "You're learning," she would say, as if Belle's survival was proof of some larger principle.

Belle stopped asking herself what she was becoming. The question felt less urgent than the next appointment, the next calculation.

What mattered was finishing the night with everything intact.

Chapter 30

The higher the rate climbed, the stranger the requests became.

Most were harmless.

Private dinners in unfamiliar cities. Long conversations about markets or art. Occasionally a weekend retreat where Belle's presence served as social camouflage.

But sometimes Celeste asked a question before confirming an appointment.

"Comfortable with travel?"

"Comfortable with extended hours?"

"Comfortable with... experimentation?"

Belle learned that "experimentation" rarely meant what men believed it meant.

It meant unpredictability.

One client requested a remote lodge in Connecticut where the nearest town was twenty minutes away. Another insisted on meetings only after midnight, claiming daylight interfered with his thinking.

"Risk has a premium," Celeste said. "But risk must remain calculable."

Belle accepted several such appointments.

The money was extraordinary.

Yet she noticed something else growing alongside the payments: an undercurrent she could not quite name.

Men who had too much power sometimes wanted proof that rules did not apply to them.

Belle began watching their hands more carefully.

Chapter 31

Pierce chose the Carlyle.

Bemelmans Bar was already settled into its evening rhythm when Belle arrived—the murals on the walls cheerful and strange, rabbits and bears moving through Central Park in painted seasons while the actual park sat dark and contained just outside. She took a corner seat where she could watch the entrance without appearing to. The piano moved through something she half-recognized.

Pierce arrived precisely on time.

He looked older than she remembered. Late fifties perhaps. His suit fit without effort, the movements of his hands precise and unhurried.

"Good evening, Belle," he said.

She smiled politely.

He gestured toward the elevator.

The suite upstairs overlooked Central Park. The park from this height was not romantic. It was a dark rectangle pressed into the grid of lights, the one wild thing the city had consented to contain. Belle noted it the way she noted most things—as information.

Pierce poured two glasses of wine and offered one.

Belle declined politely.

“I prefer clarity,” she said.

He smiled slightly.

“Celeste says you’re new.”

Belle said nothing.

Pierce watched her for a moment, the way investors watched numbers that might become trends.

“Tell me something,” he said. “Why do men pay for attention they could receive for free?”

Belle considered.

“Because attention given freely belongs to someone else.”

Pierce studied her.

"Interesting answer." He set the wine aside. "You've been trained well."

Belle let the word sit where he'd put it. *Trained.* Like a reflex. Like something done to her rather than developed by her. She did not correct him. Correction was its own kind of information.

He spoke then—about markets, about a Basquiat that had sold for more than anyone expected, about the peculiar psychology of men who controlled billions and still needed to win small arguments. Belle listened with her full attention, which was the only kind she knew how to give.

But his eyes never quite matched his voice.

The conversation was performance. The watching was the point.

Not enjoyment.

Assessment.

The lobby lights were softer now. Somewhere beyond the hallway a piano moved slowly through a familiar standard, the notes carrying just far enough to reach the elevators.

Belle crossed the marble floor without hurrying.

The doorman opened the door before she reached it.

Outside, the cold came off the park with intention. Not the cutting wind of the avenues—something quieter. The park exhaled cold the way old buildings exhaled history, steadily, without drama.

She stood under the awning for a moment.

Madison Avenue ran south in a corridor of light. Yellow taxis. Dark cars. The occasional cyclist moving against traffic with the particular confidence of someone who has decided the rules were written for other people. Across the street Central Park began—not dramatically, just a line of trees going dark above the wall, the path beyond them invisible from here.

The city at this hour had a different quality than the city at noon. The noise had not diminished. It had settled. Like a conversation that had moved past introductions into something more deliberate.

Belle had learned to read rooms.

She was beginning to read the city the same way.

She turned north and walked.

❧

When she returned to the apartment that night, Angelique stood in the kitchen with a glass of water.

"New client?" Angelique asked.

"Yes."

Angelique leaned against the counter, watching her. “Did he scare you?”

Belle considered the question.

“No,” she said slowly.

Angelique nodded.

“Those are the dangerous ones.”

Chapter 32

Celeste introduced him as Jonathan.

Not with ceremony. Simply a name written on Belle's calendar beside a dinner reservation at a quiet restaurant on the Upper East Side where the lighting softened everyone equally.

"Married," Celeste said while closing the folder.

Belle waited.

Celeste noticed that.

"Not unhappily," she added. "That distinction matters to him."

Jonathan arrived early.

He stood when Belle approached the table, which surprised her. Most men of his wealth had long ago abandoned gestures that implied effort.

"You must be Belle," he said.

His voice carried warmth rather than calculation. His suit was good but not aggressive. No visible watch. No deliberate signals of wealth.

They ordered dinner.

Jonathan spoke about books first. Not business. Not money. Books.

"Have you ever read Conrad?" he asked.

Belle shook her head.

"You might like him," Jonathan said. "He writes about people who discover too late that the map they were following was drawn by someone else."

Belle let the silence settle between them.

"That happens often," she said.

Jonathan smiled.

Over dinner, he never asked the questions most men asked—where she was from, how long she had been in New York, whether she enjoyed the work.

Instead, he asked what she noticed.

"What do you see in this room?" he said quietly.

Belle looked around.

"Three men negotiating something they don't want their wives to know about," she said.

Jonathan laughed softly.

"You're observant."

"I'm careful."

That was the first evening.

Nothing dramatic happened.

When they parted outside the restaurant, Jonathan simply said, "I'd like to see you again."

Belle felt something unfamiliar stir as she walked away.

Not attraction.

Recognition.

Chapter 33

The man Celeste's assistant showed in was not what she had expected.

Halbrecht was neither large nor imposing. He was the kind of man who had learned early that presence was more useful than size. He wore a dark suit that had not come off a rack and carried nothing—no briefcase, no folder, no phone visible. He sat down across from Celeste without being invited to and looked at her the way men looked at balance sheets.

"I appreciate your time," he said.

"Of course," Celeste replied.

He did not waste much of it.

"One of our senior partners has been a client of yours for some time," he said. "I won't pretend I don't know what the Easton Agency is."

Celeste waited.

"I don't have concerns about the arrangement itself," Halbrecht continued. "Men make choices. That's not my department."

"Then what is?" Celeste asked pleasantly.

Halbrecht studied her for a moment.

"Exposure," he said. "Specifically, whether any of your girls might at some point decide that a man in his position represents an opportunity."

Celeste allowed a brief silence before answering.

"Mr. Halbrecht," she said. "Discretion isn't a courtesy we extend. It's the architecture of everything we do. A girl who talked would never work again. In any city."

Halbrecht nodded slowly.

"And you're confident in that."

"Completely."

He seemed satisfied. Not reassured exactly—he was not a man who reassured easily—but satisfied that Celeste understood the stakes and had considered them already.

He stood.

"Then we understand each other," he said.

"We do," Celeste replied.

She walked him to the door herself. A small gesture that cost her nothing and told him everything he needed to know about how the Easton Agency was run.

After he left, she stood at the window for a moment.

Pierce was becoming expensive in ways that had nothing to do with her fees.

She filed that thought away and returned to her desk.

Chapter 34

The conversation slowed naturally.

Markets drifted into silence the way markets sometimes did when everyone already understood the outcome.

Pierce rose and crossed to the window. Central Park lay below them, winter trees dark against the pale sky.

Belle remained where she was.

"You're careful," he said.

A pause.

"You don't answer unless you have to."

"I try to be."

"Celeste teaches that."

"That's one way to learn it."

He watched her.

She held his gaze.

"Where did you learn it."

The question landed lightly.

She answered too quickly.

"Here and there."

Not much. Not enough for anyone else to notice.

But enough.

Pierce turned back toward her.

He walked across the room and stopped beside her chair.

Belle did not move.

He reached for her wrist lightly, the way a physician might confirm a pulse. The contact lasted only a moment, his thumb resting there as if measuring something invisible.

Belle held still.

Pierce watched her face.

"Good, most people reveal themselves when they think they're being admired," he said quietly.

The evening changed after that.

The conversation did not stop, but it moved closer. His questions grew shorter. His attention more deliberate.

When Belle left the Carlyle, evening had settled over the park.

The lobby lights were softer now. Somewhere beyond the hallway a piano moved slowly through a familiar standard, the notes carrying just far enough to reach the elevators.

Belle crossed the marble floor without hurrying.

The doorman opened the door before she reached it.

Cold air from the park moved cleanly through Madison Avenue.

For a moment she stood beneath the awning, watching the traffic pass between the trees.

Then she turned north.

Chapter 35

Jonathan returned a week later.

Then again later that month.

His appointments were never rushed. Never impulsive. He preferred long dinners and quiet conversation. Sometimes they walked through Central Park afterward, speaking about books or music or the peculiar loneliness of successful men.

Belle noticed something dangerous in herself.

She began looking forward to his calls.

Not for the money.

For the calm.

Jonathan never tried to purchase intimacy. He never asked questions that forced Belle to construct stories.

Instead, he listened as if her thoughts were part of the evening's architecture.

"You don't belong to this city yet," he told her once.

Belle tilted her head.

"Yet?" she asked.

"You're still measuring it," he said. "Eventually you'll stop measuring and start shaping."

The compliment unsettled her.

Meanwhile Pierce's presence grew more frequent.

His appointments were shorter. More focused. Conversations that felt less like dialogue and more like testing.

Pierce watched her constantly.

"You're becoming very valuable," he said during one meeting.

Belle did not respond.

"You know why?" he continued.

"No."

"Because you're difficult to predict."

The words sounded like praise.

They did not feel like it.

Between Jonathan's gentleness and Pierce's scrutiny, Belle felt the balance of her professional composure shifting.

The framework Celeste had built around her begun to feel... fragile.

Angelique noticed.

"You're thinking too much," she said one evening.

Belle did not deny it.

The appointment the following week was at The Mark.

Different hotel. Same floor. Pierce was already there when she arrived, which he had not been before. He stood at the window with his jacket on, no drink poured, the room carrying the particular stillness of someone who had been waiting and did not intend to show it.

"You're on time," he said.

"I'm always on time."

Pierce turned from the window.

"Sit down," he said.

The statement of a man who expected rooms to arrange themselves according to his preference.

Belle sat.

Pierce remained standing.

He crossed to the desk and lifted a folder—thin, manila, the kind that suggested its contents were more significant than its appearance. He held it for a moment without opening it.

"I'd like to ask you something," he said. "And I'd like you to answer honestly rather than strategically."

Belle waited.

"What do you know about Linebridge Capital?"

The name meant nothing. She had never heard it. But the question itself carried weight—the specific weight of something being tested rather than asked.

She understood in that moment that there was a correct answer and an honest answer and that Pierce already knew which one she would give.

"Nothing," she said.

Pierce watched her.

"You're certain."

"Yes."

He set the folder down without opening it.

"Good," he said.

He crossed to the bar and poured himself a drink, his back to her, the particular ease of a man who has just confirmed something he needed to confirm.

Belle did not ask what Linebridge was.

She filed the name the way she filed everything Pierce-adjacent—under *known*, under *later*—and kept her expression neutral and waited for the evening to resume.

Pierce turned back.

"Have you eaten?" he asked, as if the previous exchange had not occurred.

"No."

He picked up the phone and ordered dinner.

The conversation moved to other things—a board meeting in Boston, a collection he was considering acquiring, the particular tedium of men who believed their opinions about art were more interesting than their opinions about money.

Belle listened with her full attention.

She did not ask about Linebridge.

Not that evening. Not ever.

But she did not forget it either.

Later, in the elevator, she stood very still and understood what had happened.

He had not asked because he wanted information.

He had asked because he wanted to know if she would lie.

She had not.

That was the test.

She had passed it without knowing the rules.

That, she was beginning to understand, was how Pierce always ran things.

Chapter 36

The black sedan was always on the east side of the street.

Belle noticed it the third time—same plate, same tinted glass, same patient angle—and said nothing. She filed it the way Celeste had taught her to file things that could not yet be addressed. Under *known*. Under *later*.

Pierce's messages arrived the way weather arrived. Not announced. Simply present.

Seven o'clock. Carlyle.

Tonight. Different location. Car at six.

She stopped asking Celeste to confirm them.

Jonathan's messages were different. He sent them in the morning, always with a question attached, always easy to decline. *There's a restaurant on Sixty-Fourth I've been meaning to try. No obligation.* The no obligation was the tell. It was the thing Pierce would never think to say because it had never occurred to him that obligation required acknowledging.

She went to both.

One evening she left Pierce at the Carlyle at ten and found a program on her kitchen table—Phantom of the Opera, Jonathan had left it with the doorman, a single notecard tucked inside. *This was a beautiful performance.* She stood in her coat for a long moment looking at it without picking it up. The coat still smelled of Pierce's suite. The particular cold of rooms kept dark in the middle of the day.

She hung the coat in the closet.

Then she picked up the program.

The pattern settled over weeks the way debt settled—quietly, incrementally, until the weight of it was simply the new condition of things. Pierce filled the hours Pierce wanted. Jonathan filled the hours Jonathan was given. Other clients called and she did not call back, and eventually Celeste stopped scheduling them, and eventually Belle stopped noticing their absence.

"You're making yourself scarce," Celeste said one morning, her teacup raised, her eyes doing the real work.

Belle said nothing.

Celeste set the cup down. "That's an answer too."

At night she lay awake and ran the comparison the way she had learned to catalogue her wardrobe—methodically, without sentiment, setting each piece into its correct pile. Pierce: controlled, watching, each meeting a small test with no correct answer. Jonathan: present, unhurried, each evening ending with the specific ache of something she was not permitted to keep.

Both of them, in their different ways, were making her into something.

She had not yet decided if she was letting them.

One night Pierce pushed his glass aside and looked at her across the remains of dinner.

"Do you trust me?"

Belle let the silence lengthen.

"No," she said.

His smile came up slowly, like something he had been saving.

"Excellent," he said.

She understood then that this had been the test all along. Not whether she would say yes. Whether she would say no without flinching.

She had passed.

She was not sure that was good news.

Chapter 37

The text arrived at six-fifteen.

Car downstairs.

No hotel name. No time. Just the car.

Belle finished her coffee, rinsed the cup, and went downstairs.

The driver was not the one Celeste used. She noted that without reacting to it—the way she had learned to note everything Pierce-adjacent. He held the door without making eye contact. She got in.

They drove west.

When they stopped she did not recognize the building. Narrow. Glass and steel, the kind of new construction that had no history yet, only ambition. A doorman she had never seen nodded as if he knew her.

The elevator opened directly into the suite.

Pierce was already there, jacket off, a glass of wine poured and waiting on the table beside the couch. Two glasses. He gestured toward hers without looking up from his phone.

She did not sit.

On the chair beside the door sat a bag.

Her bag. The overnight one she kept on the high shelf in her closet, behind the camel coat. Packed. Zipped. Waiting with the particular patience of an object that has been handled by someone who knew exactly where to find it.

Belle looked at it for one full breath.

Then she looked at Pierce.

He had put his phone down. He was watching her the way he always watched her—not hungrily, not with heat. With the composed attention of a man waiting to see what a thing would do under pressure.

"We're going to Boston," he said. "Back Sunday."

Belle did not move.

"Celeste hasn't scheduled Boston," she said.

"No," Pierce agreed pleasantly. "She hasn't."

The room was very quiet. Somewhere below them the city moved with its usual indifference, but up here the air was still and controlled and smelled faintly of new paint.

She thought of Celeste's contract. The sentence included with deliberate precision.

No one touches you without your consent.

The bag had been touched. Her apartment had been entered. Her shelf had been reached, her things selected and folded by hands she did not know, on instructions she had not given.

None of that was in the contract.

"I'll need to speak with Celeste," Belle said.

Pierce smiled. Not the slow satisfied smile he used when she surprised him. Something more patient than that. The smile of a man who has already calculated the outcome and is simply waiting for the other party to arrive at it.

"Of course," he said.

He lifted his glass.

"There's no rush."

Belle did not reach for hers.

She stood in the room with her bag on the chair and Pierce on the couch and the city thirty floors below going about its business and understood something Celeste's training had not quite prepared her for.

Celeste had taught her to see the lines before she crossed them.

Pierce had simply moved the lines while she wasn't watching.

Chapter 38

Pierce began to change the structure of Belle's calendar, never with fanfare. Small adjustments, quietly executed. An evening appointment shifted to mid-afternoon without explanation. A dinner replaced by a quiet drink in a private club, the staff so familiar with Pierce that they blended into the walls.

Belle noticed the shifts before Celeste named them.

"He's consolidating," Celeste observed one afternoon, scanning the bookings. Her tone was neutral, eyes sharp.

Belle waited. Celeste valued patience.

"Men like Pierce prefer systems they can observe," she continued. "They don't enjoy unpredictability."

"You mean command," Belle said.

Celeste didn't correct her.

Pierce's requests increased—not daily, not frantic, but frequent enough to shift Belle's availability to close doors she hadn't realized were open. That was the complication: Pierce's patronage carried weight, not only in fees but in the invisible networks that birthed other men like him.

"Men like Pierce test structure," Celeste said.

"And if they don't respect it?" Belle asked.

Celeste paused.

"Then the structure corrects them. He is valuable," Celeste said quietly.

Belle heard the word beneath the word: useful.

"Maintain boundaries," Celeste added. "But remember the difference between firmness and provocation."

Belle nodded. She understood. In Pierce's world, boundaries were not walls. They were experiments.

Chapter 39

Jonathan never brought flowers. He brought books.

The first appeared after their third dinner—a first edition of Lord Jim, wrapped in brown paper, the receipt missing, a note inside in careful handwriting: For observation.

Belle traced the spine, recognizing the gesture for what it was. Thoughtful enough to feel personal, yet distant enough to remind her of their arrangement's limits.

Jonathan never spoke about his wife. Not directly. The absence of discussion was its own kind of presence.

One evening, as they walked along the edge of Central Park after dinner, Belle finally asked the question she'd avoided.

"Does she know?"

Jonathan gave her a faint smile. "My wife?" He stopped beside a bench, watching the city lights flicker through the trees. "My wife knows the version of me that built our life."

"And this version?" Belle asked.

He met her eyes, regret flickering there. "This version exists in quieter places."

The gifts continued—a slim volume of poetry, a small painting from a downtown gallery, a fountain pen heavy and deliberate in her hand. Each arrived without ceremony. Each one said what Jonathan would not: You matter.

And that message, so simple, produced a quiet guilt Belle had not anticipated.

Chapter 40

Belle noticed the change before Pierce said anything.

The driver had not taken them to the Carlyle.

The car stopped in front of a townhouse she did not recognize. The street was quiet, the park two blocks away, the buildings narrow and old.

Pierce stepped out first.

“You’ll like this one,” he said.

Belle did not move immediately.

“Is this where we’re meeting tonight?”

“For a while.”

Belle considered the door, the dark windows above it.

“Celeste schedules my locations,” she said.

Pierce regarded her with mild interest.

“Yes.”

The pause stretched.

Belle remained in the car.

Pierce leaned one hand on the open door.

“You’re very precise,” he said.

“I try to be.”

Another pause.

Then Pierce straightened.

"Take us to the Carlyle," he told the driver.

The car pulled away.

Inside the suite, Pierce poured wine.

"You realize," he said after a moment, "that most people would simply have come inside."

Belle watched the park through the window.

"I'm not most people."

Pierce smiled faintly.

"No," he said. "You aren't."

Chapter 41

The package arrived on a Tuesday afternoon, delivered by a courier who did not wait for signatures. Brown paper, folded precisely. No note this time, only the book itself.

The Awakening.

Belle turned it over in her hands before opening it. The cover was plain—cream paper, black lettering, the publisher's mark stamped discreetly along the spine. Inside, Jonathan had underlined nothing. No margin notes. No guidance.

He had simply sent it.

Angelique was not home. The apartment was quiet except for the distant mechanical hum of the city filtering through the windows.

Belle made tea and sat at the small table near the window.

The first chapters were easy enough—summer heat, the Gulf, a married woman drifting through a life that looked stable from the outside.

Belle read slowly.

Edna Pontellier did not seem remarkable at first. She was polite, observant, restless in a way she did not yet understand.

Belle recognized the restlessness immediately.

She read for nearly an hour before she realized she had stopped turning pages and was staring at a single line.

A certain light was beginning to dawn dimly within her.

Belle closed the book halfway.

Outside, Manhattan moved with the same quiet machinery it always had—taxis, distant sirens, the low friction of traffic moving through wet pavement.

Edna had a husband.

Jonathan had a wife.

The symmetry was not subtle.

Belle reopened the book and read further.

The man in the story—Robert—was attentive without claiming anything. Gentle. Curious. Present in ways that did not threaten the architecture surrounding them.

Belle knew that type of man.

Jonathan listened the same way.

He never pushed. Never asked questions that forced decisions. He occupied space beside her instead of rearranging it.

It was easy to imagine how a woman might mistake that for something permanent.

Belle reached the chapter where Edna first realizes the danger of what she is feeling.

She stopped again.

The danger wasn't the man.

It was the recognition.

Belle leaned back in the chair, the book resting lightly against her knee.

Jonathan would never ask her to leave.

He would never ask for anything that large.

He would simply continue appearing—dinners, books, quiet weekends that felt almost like ordinary life.

That was the problem.

Ordinary life was not available to either of them.

She closed the book and looked out the window.

The city did not pause for awakenings.

It moved forward with the same untroubled rhythm, indifferent to the private revolutions occurring inside apartments.

Belle ran her thumb along the edge of the pages.

Jonathan had not marked the passages he wanted her to notice.

He trusted her to find them herself.

That thought stayed with her longer than the story.

Chapter 42

The car arrived without notice.

Belle noticed the difference immediately. Celeste's appointments always arrived through the calendar—clean entries, a driver's name, a hotel she had seen before. This one appeared as a text.

Driver waiting downstairs.

No location.

Belle stared at the screen for a moment before dressing.

When she reached the curb, the car door opened automatically. The driver did not speak. He handed her an envelope containing a key card and a room number.

The sky to the west had gone the color of old iron. The kind of sky that didn't announce itself—it simply arrived and waited for everything beneath it to understand.

The building was not a hotel.

A residential tower near the river—new construction, glass and marble, the lobby unfinished enough that the security desk looked temporary.

Pierce stood inside the apartment when she entered.

The room had been stripped of hospitality: no dinner table, staff, or bar cart. Just a large empty living room overlooking the water.

"You're early," he said.

Belle set her coat on the back of a chair that had clearly been brought into the room for the occasion.

"You changed the venue," she said.

Pierce nodded as if that were obvious.

"I prefer variation."

Belle remained standing.

Silence stretched between them.

Pierce walked toward the window, studying the skyline as if he had invited her there only to share the view.

"You've been difficult lately," he said.

Belle did not answer.

Pierce turned back.

"You decline extensions. You limit availability." His tone was almost conversational. "Celeste finds it admirable."

Belle said nothing.

"But admiration," he continued, "is not the same as usefulness."

He crossed the room toward her.

Moving through the space the way men moved through space when they had never learned to consider whether they were welcome in it.

He stopped closer than he should have.

Almost touching but not quite. Simply there—near enough that she could smell the faint cedar of his jacket, near enough that moving back would have been a statement.

Belle did not move back.

Pierce studied her face the way he studied everything—not hungrily, not with heat, but with the patient attention of a man cataloguing something he expected to own eventually.

"Do you know why I continue seeing you?" he asked.

She kept her voice level. "You enjoy conversation."

"No."

He didn't move. Didn't shift his weight. The stillness was the point—the absolute ease of a man who had never once, in his life, worried that he was standing somewhere he shouldn't be.

Belle felt the old reflex: soften it, smile, give him something so he would step back. She recognized it the way she recognized a road she'd driven badly before.

She said nothing.

Pierce tilted his head slightly.

"You're doing something," he said. "Right now."

"Am I."

"Deciding whether to manage me." He almost smiled. "Most women have decided by now. You're still running the calculation."

Belle met his eyes.

"The calculation isn't finished," she said.

Pierce nodded, as if she'd confirmed something.

"Good," he said.

Thunder moved through the building from somewhere across the river—low, unhurried, felt more than heard, the way certain things arrive.

He stepped back—unhurried, untroubled—and returned to the window.

Belle's pulse had not slowed. She was not sure when it had quickened.

That was the part she would remember later.
Not his proximity or his words.
The fact that she hadn't felt it happen.

Chapter 43

Celeste listened without interruption.

Belle finished speaking and waited.

The townhouse was quiet except for the faint clink of Celeste setting her teacup down.

"He tested a boundary," Celeste said finally.

"He crossed it."

"No," Celeste replied calmly. "He approached it."

Belle felt the anger return.

"He threatened me. Just not with words"

Celeste met her eyes.

"And when you asked him to stop?"

"He did."

Celeste nodded once.

"That distinction matters."

Belle stared at her.

"You told me no one would touch me without permission."

Celeste did not flinch.

"And he did not."

The logic was precise.

And unbearable.

Belle stood.

"I'm done. I mean it. I'm not—

"You may decline," she said.

Belle waited.

"But understand the consequence."

Belle knew before Celeste said it.

"Pierce represents a significant amount of the agency's annual revenue."

The sentence sat between them like an object.

Celeste's voice remained calm.

"I will support whatever decision you make."

Belle said nothing.

After a moment Celeste added quietly:

"However, men like Pierce rarely tolerate abrupt rejection. If you disappear, his curiosity becomes resentment."

Belle crossed her arms.

"So, what do you want me to do?"

Celeste's answer came without hesitation.

"Control the terms."

Belle understood the translation.

See him again.

But on her terms.

The silence stretched long enough that Celeste finally spoke again.

"You are not prey," she said.

Belle looked at the floor and back to Celeste.

The statement felt uncertain.

Chapter 44

Jonathan's invitation arrived unexpectedly.

"Come with me," he said one evening after dinner.

"To where?"

"Vermont," he answered. "A house I use sometimes."

Belle didn't respond right away. Travel with clients was not unusual, but Jonathan's tone was different. Careful in a new way. As if he had been carrying the question for some time and had finally decided the weight of it wasn't worth the carrying.

"This isn't work," he said quietly.

She almost laughed. "It's always work," she replied.

Jonathan accepted that without argument.

And still, the trip happened.

The house sat above a hillside already deep into its turning—maples gone red at the edges, birches yellow and shaking, the sky above them that particular blue that only appears when the air has gone cold enough to be honest. The driveway was gravel and pine needles. The house itself was old, white clapboard, a porch that wrapped around two sides. Not a showpiece. A place that had been used and cared for over many years by people who knew how.

Belle stepped out of the car and stood still for a moment.

She had not heard silence like this since Mississippi. But it was a different kind of silence. Yazoo City's silence waited. This one simply was.

Jonathan carried both bags inside without asking.

The kitchen smelled of woodsmoke and something faintly herbal—dried bundles hung above the window over the sink, sage or thyme, the kind of detail that accumulated over decades rather than being arranged. He moved through the space with the ease of a man who did not have to think about where anything was. Opened a cabinet without looking. Knew which burner ran hot.

Belle sat at the kitchen table and watched him cook.

It was the watching that undid her, slightly.

Not desire. Something quieter and more dangerous. The way he filled an ordinary room. The particular competence of someone who had learned to take care of themselves and then, somewhere along the way, had begun to take care of others so naturally he no longer noticed doing it.

"You look comfortable here," she said.

"I am," Jonathan said.

He did not elaborate. He didn't need to.

They ate at the kitchen table with the windows going dark around them and the candles doing what candles do to a room. They talked about books and then about the places books had taken them as children and then, without quite deciding to, about the strange loneliness of people who had built successful lives and discovered that success did not solve the particular problem of being alone in a room with your own thoughts.

Jonathan refilled her glass without asking.

She did not stop him.

Later they sat on the porch in the cold with blankets across their laps and the dark pressing in from the tree line, and Belle felt something she had not felt in a long time—possibly ever. Not safety exactly. Not happiness. Something more like *suspension*. The feeling of a life paused at its best possible moment before it was required to continue.

She thought, *I could stay here.*

She let herself think it.

Just that once.

❧

In the morning Jonathan was gone before she woke.

A note on the kitchen table. *Back by two. Coffee's made.*

She drank it alone at the table with the windows full of morning light and the hills beyond them impossible colors and the house entirely quiet around her. His coffee cup was already washed and sitting upside down on the rack. She had not heard him leave.

She found a book on the side table near the couch—not one he had brought for her, just one that lived there, its spine bent to a particular page as if someone had set it face down too many times in the same spot. She read for two hours without moving.

This was what it would be, she thought. If it were anything.

Mornings like this. Coffee made. The particular smell of a house that knew how to be a house.

She closed the book carefully and put it back where she'd found it.

❧

Jonathan returned at half past two.

He came through the door with the particular brightness of a man glad to be back somewhere, and then—in the space of crossing the threshold—something adjusted in him. Not extinguishing. Dimming. The way a man dims when he remembers what room he's in and what room he's supposed to be in and that those are not the same room.

Belle saw it happen.

She did not say anything.

He made tea. Asked how she'd spent the morning. Listened to her answer. Everything was the same. Everything was slightly different.

That evening dinner was quieter. Not unhappy. Just honest. The suspension had ended and ordinary time had resumed and in ordinary time Jonathan had a life that contained her only in these careful intervals.

On the drive back to the city, he was warm and present and entirely himself.

But the house was already receding behind them.

And Belle understood—not with anger, not yet with grief, but with the clean clear knowledge of someone who has finally looked at a thing directly—that this was the whole of it.

Mornings he was gone before she woke.

Evenings that dimmed when he crossed the threshold.

A life with two versions. And the second version—the real one, the structural one, the one built from obligation and money and a marriage that was also a corporation—that version always came first.

She did not say this aloud.

She watched the highway and let Vermont become memory, which was the only thing it had ever really been.

The week after Vermont, Belle moved through the apartment carefully, the way you move through a space when something in it has shifted and you haven't yet identified what. Work continued. Appointments held. Celeste's messages were answered promptly, Betsy's calls with the right amount of warmth. Vermont stayed off to one side, not ignored exactly, but avoided the way you avoid a bruise—aware of its location, careful not to press.

Jonathan's message arrived on Thursday morning, the way his messages always arrived. *There's a path along the Pond I've been meaning to show you. No obligation.*

She read it twice.

Then she put on her coat.

Chapter 45

Pierce began sending messages directly.

Not through the agency phone.

Short messages.

Precise.

Available tomorrow.

Dinner moved.

Same place.

The first time it happened, Belle ignored it.

Celeste noticed immediately.

"He shouldn't be contacting you directly," Celeste said, studying the screen.

"Do you want me to block him?"

Celeste shook her head slowly.

"No."

That was the answer.

Pierce's messages continued.

They never contained flirtation. Never anything overtly personal. Only instructions disguised as requests.

One evening after dinner he walked Belle to the elevator and said quietly:

"I prefer communication without intermediaries."

Belle waited.

"That complicates things," she replied.

Pierce smiled.

"Complication is where information lives."

Belle understood the implication.

He wasn't pursuing intimacy.

He was narrowing the system.

Chapter 46

The city softened inside the park.

Belle crossed Fifth Avenue just after four and stepped through the stone arch at Sixty-Fourth Street. The traffic noise dropped behind her as if someone had closed a door. Gravel paths curved away under long rows of elms, their branches stretching overhead like the ribs of a cathedral. The late afternoon light filtered through leaves that had begun to yellow at the edges, turning the air a quiet gold.

Central Park did not belong to Manhattan. It belonged to the idea of Manhattan—a pause large enough to make the buildings look temporary.

Jonathan stood near the path that led toward the Pond, one hand in the pocket of his coat. He had chosen a charcoal jacket that made him look slightly younger than he was. Or perhaps it was the park that did that—the illusion that people walking here were simply people and not collections of obligations.

"You found it," he said when he saw her.

"I followed the trees."

He smiled at that and fell into step beside her.

They walked without speaking at first. The path curved along the water where the Pond held the reflection of the skyline like something borrowed. Ducks cut quiet wakes through the surface. Across the bridge, a violinist played for no one in particular, the notes drifting between the trees as if the park itself had decided to hum.

"You come here often?" Belle asked.

"Less than I should," Jonathan said. "New York trains you to forget it's here."

They passed a woman throwing a tennis ball for a dog that seemed convinced the game would end if it stopped running. A pair of students sat cross-legged on the grass with a sketchbook open between them. A man in running shoes moved past them in long, silent strides.

Belle watched it all with the particular attention she had learned to give rooms.

"No one is looking," she said quietly.

Jonathan glanced at her.

"Looking at what?"

"At anything," she said.

He followed her gaze around the path. People moved through the park the way water moved around stones—adjusting without comment.

"That's why people come here," he said. "It's the only place in the city where you can pretend not to matter."

Belle considered that.

"Does it work?"

"Sometimes."

They crossed Bow Bridge slowly, the iron railings warm from the afternoon sun. From the center of the span the lake opened beneath them, green and still. The buildings along Central Park West rose beyond the trees in quiet tiers of glass and limestone.

Jonathan rested his hands on the railing.

He was quiet for a moment before he spoke. Below them the lake held the last of the afternoon light, the water going dark at the edges where the shadow of the bridge fell across it.

Belle looked toward the near bank.

On the elm closest to the water, just above the waterline where the bark had gone smooth with age, a Luna Moth rested with its wings spread flat against the wood. Impossibly green. The size of a man's hand. Its long hindwing tails curved downward like something calligraphic, and on each wing a single eyespot looked outward at the park with the patient, unblinking attention of something that had been here longer than the bridge.

Belle stared at it.

Her heart lifted once, briefly, the way it lifted for things that had no business being where they were and were there anyway.

In Mississippi Luna Moths came in May, sometimes June, drawn to porch lights and gas station fluorescents, their wings the color of new cotton leaves. She had not seen one since she left.

She had not expected to see one here.

Jonathan was still speaking. She heard him—the company, the shares, the structure of a life built on someone else's foundation—and she listened, but part of her stayed on the moth. On the eyespots that were not eyes. On the wings that said *look here* so you would not look at what was underneath.

She understood that principle.

She had been practicing it for years.

The moth did not move.

When Belle looked back at Jonathan he had finished speaking and was watching her with the expression of a man who has just said something true and is waiting to see what it costs him.

She looked back at the elm.

The moth was gone.

"I had my first real kiss on this bridge," he said.

Belle turned slightly toward him. "How old were you?"

"Seventeen."

"That seems late."

"My parents were... careful people."

Belle smiled faintly.

"I can't imagine you being careful."

"You should have met me then."

The wind lifted briefly across the water, carrying the smell of leaves and damp stone. For a moment neither of them spoke.

Belle felt the strange calm she sometimes felt with him—not the practiced composure Celeste had taught her, but something older and less deliberate.

He had never treated her like an arrangement.

He treated her like a woman who happened to exist.

That difference had begun quietly, months ago. A dinner that ran long. A conversation that moved from books to childhood to the way people changed when money entered the room.

She had tried to keep the distance Celeste required.

It had not worked.

Jonathan spoke again without turning.

"I should tell you something," he said.

Belle felt the shift immediately. Not in his words—in the air around them. The wind had picked up.

"What is it."

He watched a rowboat drift beneath the bridge before answering.

"My wife's family," he said slowly, "is where the money comes from."

Belle waited.

"Her father built the company," Jonathan continued. "The real one. The one people think I run."

"And you don't?"

"I run the visible part," he said. "Boards. Acquisitions. Meetings that last three hours and accomplish nothing."

He smiled without humor.

"But the shares," he added. "Those belong to them."

Belle rested her elbows on the railing beside him.

"So, you married the company."

"In a way."

"And you can't leave."

Jonathan did not answer immediately.

A boy somewhere in the park shouted with the triumph of someone who had just caught a ball.

"No," Jonathan said finally. "I can't."

Belle had already known that.

Not the mechanics of it—the shares, the configuration—but the shape of the answer.

Men like Jonathan did not arrive in quiet restaurants on Madison Avenue by accident. Their lives were built from agreements older than their marriages.

Still, hearing it spoken placed the truth somewhere solid.

"And if you did?" she asked.

He turned then and looked at her fully.

"I would lose everything."

"Everything."

"The company," he said. "The house in Connecticut. Most of the board seats. A great deal of money."

Belle watched him with the same calm she had learned to bring to negotiations.

"And your wife?"

Jonathan looked back at the lake.

"My wife," he said carefully, "is part of the structure."

Belle felt the sentence settle.

Not cruel. Not tender. Only accurate.

The violinist had moved closer now. The music drifted across the bridge in slow phrases that rose and fell like breath.

"Why are you telling me this?" she asked.

Jonathan considered that for a moment.

"Because I suspect," he said quietly, "that you're intelligent enough to ask the question eventually."

Belle looked out across the park.

The trees had begun to turn. Yellow first, then rust along the edges. Autumn in New York did not arrive gradually. It declared itself.

"I already knew," she said.

Jonathan raised an eyebrow slightly.

"You did?"

"Not the details," Belle said. "But the outcome."

"And what outcome is that."

She turned toward him.

"That you are not someone I can have."

The words surprised him. She could see it in the brief stillness that followed.

"You make that sound very final."

"It is."

"Does that bother you."

Belle thought about that honestly.

Weeks ago, the answer might have been yes.

Now she understood something Celeste had been trying to teach her.

People were rarely free in the ways they imagined.

"No," she said.

Jonathan watched her with a new kind of attention.

"Why not."

"Because now I know the rules," Belle said.

The wind moved again through the trees.

Below them the rowboats shifted gently against their ropes.

Jonathan studied her face as if searching for something he had expected to find there and did not.

"You're remarkable," he said finally.

Belle shook her head slightly.

"No," she said.

"What then."

She looked out over the park one last time before answering.

"Just observant."

They walked back toward Fifth Avenue as the sun dropped behind the buildings.

The city waited beyond the trees exactly where they had left it.

Chapter 47

Angelique was used to unusual requests.

Not dangerous exactly.

Specific.

Clients asked about experiences beyond the usual contract terms. Curiosity wrapped in polite language.

One evening she mentioned it casually in the apartment kitchen.

"Men read too much," she said, pouring a glass of water.

Belle looked up.

"What kind of requests?"

Angelique shrugged.

"Control."

Belle understood the word immediately.

Celeste had rules.

Strict ones.

No restraints. No marks. No activities that could produce evidence.

Anything beyond that required negotiation.

Angelique handled such negotiations herself.

"You say no?" Belle asked.

"Usually."

"And the rest?"

Angelique sipped her water.

"The rest depends on the client."

Chapter 48

She opened the notebook Jonathan had sent with the fountain pen and began to write.

I'm not certain whether this is a letter or simply a way of putting a thought somewhere outside my own head.

You have been careful with me. I noticed that from the beginning. Most men arrive with curiosity or entitlement or a need to prove something. You arrived with attention. That is rarer than people think.

The books were a kindness. Not because of the objects themselves, but because they suggested that you believed I would read them. That assumption carried more respect than many compliments I have heard.

Central Park felt almost like another city. People walking dogs, students sketching, a violin drifting across the bridge as if the afternoon had decided to make music. For a moment it was possible to imagine that we were simply two people who had met there by accident.

But imagination is not the same thing as truth.

You once told me that Conrad wrote about people discovering too late that the map they followed was drawn by someone else. I think the more difficult discovery is realizing that the map is correct and choosing not to follow it anyway.

Your life is already built. You were honest about that without needing to say it directly. I respect the honesty.

I also understand the outline of things now well enough to know that what we share exists only in the quiet spaces between obligations. Those spaces are real, but they are not foundations.

You have been good to me in the ways that were possible. I will remember that without bitterness.

But I think it is better if we do not see each other again.

Not because anything was wrong.

Because too much of it was right.

Belle

She folded the pages carefully and placed them in the small drawer of the writing desk beside the books Jonathan had sent her. Then she closed it and did not open it again.

❧

She saw Angelique as she stepped into the kitchen.

"Men like Jonathan fall in love with women they can't have," Angelique said.

Belle set the kettle on the stove.

"Some women do that too."

Chapter 49

Celeste reviewed the file herself.

Investment banking. Married. No litigation history. Three independent channels of verification, each returning clean. The kind of client the agency had built its reputation on—predictable, discreet, expensive in the right ways.

She initialed the bottom of the page.

The screening process existed because Celeste believed in architecture. Not rules—rules could be argued with. Architecture simply was. You built the structure correctly and the structure held. She had been building it for fifteen years. It held because she was careful about what went into it.

She closed the folder.

The appointment was standard. Dinner. Two hours. No marks. Angelique had handled this profile dozens of times. She was the most capable woman in the agency—composed, precise, the kind of woman who read a room before she fully entered it. If Celeste trusted anyone to manage a client correctly, it was Angelique.

She set the folder on the corner of her desk where her assistant would collect it.

"Remember the margins," she said when Angelique came to collect it.

Angelique inclined her head.

"I always do."

Celeste watched her leave.

The system was working exactly as it was supposed to.

Chapter 50

The message arrived in the car, after the confirmation text had already been sent.

There's something else I'd like.

Angelique read it once. Then again.

Breath control. Carotid pressure. He used the language of safety—duration limits, release signals, the vocabulary of someone who had read carefully and believed reading was the same as knowing.

She deleted the message.

Outside, the city moved past the window with its usual indifference. She watched a woman cross against the light without breaking stride, a man in a dark coat folding his newspaper against the wind, a cab cutting across two lanes because it could.

She had done it before. Not often. Not carelessly. The margin between ten seconds and twelve was not large, but it was real, and she had always respected it.

She thought about Celeste's contract. The sentence included with deliberate precision.

No one touches you without your consent.

The contract ran in one direction. This ran in the other. She would be the one deciding.

She pressed two fingers briefly to her sternum—the old signal, the one that meant *you go, you don't calculate, you just go*—and held them there for a moment.

Then she let her hand fall.

The car turned onto the block where the hotel stood, its awning lit against the dark.

Angelique looked at her reflection in the window.

She had always trusted her own margins.

Chapter 51

Dinner first. Conversation ordinary.

The request returned over cleared plates.

"This would be off the clock," he said.

"And an extra fifteen hundred," she said.

He agreed.

She explained the mechanics. Carotid compression, not airway restriction. Hands at the sides of the neck. Ten seconds maximum. Two taps and he released immediately. He repeated the instructions back to her. His hands were steady. His voice was controlled. He had done his reading.

It began precisely.

There is a difference between restricting breath and restricting blood. Breath burns. Blood simply vanishes.

Her signal was to tap twice.

He felt her hands move and believed it was part of the choreography.

He held for two seconds longer than he should have. Perhaps three.

When he released her she did not collapse. She simply did not correct herself.

He spoke her name once. Then again.

There was breath. Shallow. Irregular.

He believed she would recover.

When she did not open her eyes he called Celeste.

"There's been an accident."

Celeste's voice did not change.

"Is she conscious?"

"No."

"Is she breathing?"

"I think so."

"Stay where you are. Do not leave."

❧

By the time the physician arrived the shallow breath had stopped.

Carotid compression can interrupt the heart without bruising the skin. The body does not always announce the injury.

Time of death was recorded quietly.

The suite was vacated before sunrise.

The official cause would not reference him.

Angelique's family would receive a different version.

Chapter 52

When Belle was called to the townhouse the next morning, Celeste stood at the window with her back to the room. She did not turn immediately.

"There was an incident," Celeste said. "Angelique accepted terms beyond protocol."

Belle felt the floor tilt beneath her.

"She's dead?"

The word came out raw, stripped of everything except the question.

Celeste finally turned. Her face was composed, but her eyes were not.

"Yes."

Belle stood very still. The single word landed like a weight dropped into still water—slow, heavy, spreading outward until it filled the entire room.

"How?"

Celeste did not soften it.

"She allowed control to exceed structure."

"She understood the risk."

That was the only explanation she offered.

Belle stood very still. The words moved through her like something physical, slow and heavy. She felt the floor beneath her feet, the particular coolness of the marble, the faint smell of citrus from the diffuser on the side table. Everything was the same as it had been yesterday. And nothing was.

She did not cry in that room.

Later, alone in the apartment, Belle stood in the hallway outside Angelique's door.

It was closed.

She did not open it.

Instead, she looked at the shoes Angelique had left by the threshold—angled the way she always left them, not quite together, not quite apart, as if she had stepped out of them mid-thought and would be back in a moment to decide whether they were right for the evening.

Belle stood there long enough that the city outside stopped registering. Cars honking, jackhammers, workmen shouting—all gone. Just the hallway and the shoes and the particular silence of a room that did not yet know no one was coming back to it.

She went to the kitchen instead and stood at the counter with both hands flat against the marble, looking at nothing until she could breathe evenly again.

As the news filtered through the agency, so did the others.

They came quietly, one by one, carrying nothing but themselves. No one brought flowers. No one brought food. They simply arrived and filled the spaces Angelique had once filled with her laugh, her easy confidence, her particular way of moving through a room as if she had already decided life would be interesting.

Sofia cried in the kitchen without sound.

Leila sat on the edge of the couch and stared at the floor.

Mei stood by the window with her arms crossed, as if holding something fragile inside her chest.

No one spoke much.

Celeste moved among them with the same quiet efficiency she brought to everything. She canceled appointments. She rerouted phones. She spoke in low, precise sentences about what would and would not be said.

Belle watched her and felt something cold settle in her stomach.

Later that night, when the others had gone, Belle returned to the hallway.

She still did not open Angelique's door.

She simply stood there until the silence became too loud, then went to her own room and lay down fully clothed on top of the covers.

She did not sleep.

She thought about the last time she had seen Angelique laugh—head thrown back, eyes bright, saying something about how ridiculous men were when they thought they were in control.

Belle pressed the heels of her hands into her eyes until sparks flashed behind the lids.

She did not cry then either.

The grief came later, in small, unexpected waves—when she reached for the coffee mug Angelique always used, when she caught the faint trace of jasmine in the bathroom, when she realized the apartment would never again sound the way it had when two people lived in it.

Some losses did not arrive all at once.

They arrived in pieces, and you carried each one separately.

❧

She tried to remember everything she actually knew about Angelique.

She knew Angelique had grown up in Detroit, but she never said much about it except once, when she mentioned that her mother had worked two jobs and still made Sunday dinner every week. She knew Angelique had a younger brother she sent money to, but she never showed pictures. She knew Angelique had been in New York for four years before Belle arrived, and that she had chosen the name Angelique herself because she liked how it sounded when said slowly.

She knew Angelique didn't like roses but loved peonies. She knew Angelique could make a room feel warmer just by walking into it, but she could also make it feel colder if she decided you were wasting her time. She knew Angelique kept a small leather journal locked in the bottom drawer of her nightstand, but Belle had never seen inside it. She knew Angelique had once said, quietly, after too much wine, "I don't want anyone to ever feel sorry for me. Not even you."

And she knew that Angelique had been the first person in New York who looked at her—really looked—and said, "You're not as soft as you pretend to be. That's going to save you one day."

Belle pressed her forehead against her knees.

She had never asked the important questions. Where did you learn to move like that? What scared you? Who were you before you became Angelique?

Now those questions would stay unanswered forever.

The silence in the apartment felt heavier than it ever had.

Chapter 53

Celeste Voss believed in systems.

Grief did not change that.

By ten o'clock the machinery of containment was already in motion.

Phones were rerouted. Schedules erased. Clients contacted with quiet explanations about unforeseen circumstances.

A lawyer was on retainer for situations exactly like this.

Celeste moved through the agency office like a conductor guiding a silent orchestra.

She did not raise her voice. She did not show panic. But every woman in the room understood the seriousness of the moment.

The rules were simple.

No one spoke to reporters.

No one speculated.

No one posted anything online.

Angelique's name was not to appear anywhere near the agency.

Belle watched all of this from the doorway.

The efficiency made her stomach twist.

"How can you do this?" Belle asked.

Celeste looked up from a folder.

"Do what?"

"Act like this is... logistics."

Celeste closed the folder slowly.

"This is logistics."

"She was my friend."

Celeste's expression softened slightly.

"Yes."

"Then why are you talking about liability?"

Celeste studied Belle for a long moment.

Because someone had to.

But she didn't say that.

Instead, she walked toward Belle.

"You think this is cold," Celeste said.

Belle didn't answer.

"It isn't."

Celeste's voice dropped.

"It's how I keep the rest of you alive."

Belle looked away.

Celeste touched her arm briefly.

"I am grieving too," she said quietly.

Belle wanted to believe that.

But Celeste's composure was so perfect it felt impossible.

Chapter 54

Belle waited until evening before opening Angelique's door.

The hallway felt longer than it ever had before.

Her hand hovered over the knob.

Then she turned it.

The room smelled faintly of jasmine and expensive soap.

Everything was exactly where Angelique had left it.

Her silk robe hung from the back of a chair. Books stacked neatly on the nightstand. Lipstick on the dresser.

Ordinary things.

Belle stepped inside slowly.

The silence pressed in from every direction.

She sat on the edge of the bed.

She rubbed her neck absentmindedly, the way she did when the tension refused to leave her shoulders.

Angelique had always filled a room with energy—her voice, her

laughter, the way she moved like someone who had already decided life would be interesting.

Now the room held only absence.

Belle picked up a small silver mirror from the dresser. Angelique had once said, half joking, "Beauty is armor. Never forget that."

Belle pressed the mirror to her chest and closed her eyes. “I’m sorry,” she whispered.

But the room did not answer.

Chapter 55

They gathered after midnight.

Six women around Celeste's dining table.

No clients. No phones. No schedules.

Just candles.

One by one they lit them.

Angelique had always loved rituals. Small private ceremonies that gave shape to things too big for words.

Celeste poured wine.

No one drank.

Finally Celeste spoke.

"We will remember her tonight," she said.

Silence followed.

Then Sofia began to cry softly.

Belle tried to speak.

But when she opened her mouth nothing came out.

Her throat closed around the words.

Celeste reached across the table and squeezed her hand.

For the first time that night, Celeste's voice wavered.

"She was extraordinary," she said quietly.

The candlelight flickered as if an invisible breeze had passed through the room.

And for a moment the room held something fragile and sacred.

Chapter 56

Belle tried to write the letter three times.

Dear Mr. and Mrs.—

She stopped.

What could she possibly say?

Your daughter died in a Manhattan apartment because she trusted the wrong man.

Belle crumpled the paper.

The trash can filled with half-written pages.

Finally, she sat back in the chair and stared at the blank sheet.

"I loved her," Belle whispered.

The words hung in the room.

Simple. True.

But still not enough.

Chapter 57

The apartment did not change.

The couch remained square against the wall. The two identical lamps still cast the same restrained light across the narrow living room. The refrigerator hummed with the same quiet efficiency. Celeste's system had not been designed to register grief.

Only the silence was different.

Belle noticed it most in the mornings. Angelique used to move through the kitchen with small sounds—water running, a cabinet closing, the low scrape of a chair against tile. None of it had been loud. But together it had created proof of another life moving nearby.

Now the apartment held only Belle's breathing.

The second bedroom door remained closed. Celeste had not reassigned it yet. The bed inside was made too tightly, the way Angelique always left it. A glass sat upside down on the bathroom counter, exactly where she had placed it the last morning she left.

Belle had not moved it.

Celeste had visited two days after the funeral.

Not to mourn.

To stabilize.

"You will continue," Celeste said from the kitchen table, reviewing a slim folder. "The agency cannot pause for sentiment."

Belle had expected that.

Still, hearing it spoken aloud clarified something.

Angelique had been the human side of the system. Celeste was its architecture.

"What happened?" Belle asked quietly.

Celeste did not answer immediately. She closed the folder.

"A miscalculation," she said.

That was all.

No details. No explanation of the client involved. No apology.

Belle understood the rule in that moment.

What happened to Angelique belonged to the system now, not to the girls who had known her.

The next week moved forward without ceremony.

Appointments resumed.

The car arrived on time.

The hotels were the same.

But Belle noticed something subtle shifting in the behavior of the other women.

They were polite.

They were professional.

But conversations shortened. Phone calls ended quickly. The quiet community that had existed around Angelique—shared warnings, quiet advice, the occasional glass of wine—dissolved.

Not out of cruelty.

Out of instinct.

Grief was inefficient.

Celeste had introduced a new phrase during their next meeting.

"Risk tolerance."

Belle sat across from her in the townhouse on East Seventy-Sixth while Celeste explained adjustments to scheduling, screening, and travel.

"We are not reducing activity," Celeste said calmly. "We are refining the margins."

Belle listened.

The language sounded identical to the conversations Pierce had described about financial markets.

Exposure.

Mitigation.

Containment.

Human lives translated into management.

"Are the clients aware?" Belle asked.

Celeste's mouth tilted faintly.

"They are always aware," she said. "That is why they pay."

When Belle returned to the hallway later, she paused outside Angelique's closed door.

For a moment she considered opening it.

Instead, she continued past.

The structure remained intact.

Only the person who had taught her how to survive inside it was gone.

And, without Angelique, Belle felt the system around her without the buffer of someone who understood it.

It was colder than she remembered.

Chapter 58

Belle left Manhattan before sunrise.

The city was quiet in that strange hour before traffic and noise returned.

She flew south.

By noon she was walking the streets of the French Quarter. In a way, Belle Devereaux had been born here. Not Annabelle, but Belle.

St. Louis Cathedral overshadowed Jackson Square, its grand façade towering behind the gardens as if designed to highlight its majestic presence. Vendors displayed their paintings on the wrought iron fence. A man, painted entirely in silver, stood impossibly still with a hat at his feet to collect tips. A woman had just finished setting up a table with a deck of tarot cards. New Orleans never changed, and Belle relied on that stability.

Royal Street smelled the same as always—coffee, humidity, old wood. She turned right at Dumaine.

The small shop still sat between two narrow galleries.

Belle pushed open the door.

Wind chimes rattled softly.

Inside, the shop smelled of incense and candle wax.

The old woman behind the counter looked up.

"You been here before, you," she said.

Belle nodded.

It seemed years ago.

Before New York.

Before Angelique.

Before everything.

Her eyes moved across the shelves until she found it.

A small silver moth pendant hanging from a black cord.

The same symbol as the tattoo on her wrist.

Transformation.

Fragile wings moving toward light.

Belle held it in her palm.

"How much?" she asked.

The woman studied her.

"Mais, ma chérie." She tilted her head, soft. "You already pay for dat. Long time ago, you pay." Belle frowned.

But the woman only smiled.

"Some t'ings, dey wait. Dey wait till you ready to carry dem again."

Belle slipped the pendant around her neck.

The metal was cool when she picked it up. By the time it settled against her collarbone it was warmer than her skin. Warmer than the room.

She stood with her hand flat against it for a moment.

Then she stepped back into the street.

For the first time in days, she breathed deeply.

Outside, the afternoon sun warmed the narrow street.

At a small jeweler's on the corner, she stopped and bought a sterling silver chain—something permanent, something hers. She stood on the sidewalk and made the transfer, slipping the black cord into her pocket like she was setting something down.

She walked to Café Du Monde and ordered beignets. The sun was warm, and she found a pleasant shady spot near the edge of the canopy. She picked up the book Jonathan had sent and read more about Edna Pontellier. Edna had walked into the water because she couldn't find a way to own the shore. Belle looked at the Mississippi River and didn't see a grave; she saw a shipping lane.

Chapter 59

The air in New York was different than the air in New Orleans. In the Quarter, the atmosphere was a soup of history and humidity—it clung to your skin like a damp wool blanket, heavy with the scent of jasmine and rot. New York air was filtered, recycled, and sharp. It tasted of ozone and expensive limestone.

She went to her apartment first.

The hallway smelled the same. Angelique's door was closed. The glass still sat upside down on the bathroom counter exactly where she had left it.

Belle set her bag down and stood for a moment in the particular silence of a place that had been empty and knew it.

She went to the bathroom.

Reached for the brush automatically, the way you reach for something you have reached for every morning for years without thinking about it.

The shelf was bare where it had been.

She checked the drawer beneath. The cabinet above. The edge of the sink.

Gone.

She stood there for a moment.

Then she filed it the way she filed things she couldn't yet address.

Under *known*. Under *later*.

She picked up her bag—good leather, no hardware, the kind of thing that didn't announce itself—and walked to the townhouse.

Belle stood in the entry of the townhouse for a full minute before calling upstairs. She felt the weight of the moth pendant against her collarbone. It was cool to the touch, a heavy anchor of nickel painted silver that seemed to pulse with the rhythm of her heart.

Some things come back when you're ready, the woman had said.

Belle wasn't just ready. She was inevitable.

She walked up the stairs to Celeste's private office. The rest of the townhouse was all restraint—white walls, bare surfaces, nothing that didn't earn its place. But Celeste's private office was different. Books she had actually read, their spines cracked and annotated. A small painting that was probably significant to someone who would know. Photographs, a few of them personal. A lamp with an amber shade that made the light feel almost warm. It was the room of a woman who had built herself carefully and then, in here, allowed herself to be interested in things.

Belle stood in the doorway for a moment.

She had not expected this.

Celeste was at her desk, afternoon light coming in behind her through windows that looked out over the street below. She didn't look up immediately. She was a woman who used silence as a measuring stick.

"You're late," Celeste said, her voice like a dry martini.

"I'm exactly when I meant to be," Belle replied.

Celeste froze. It wasn't the words; it was the cadence. The Mississippi lilt was still there, but the apology that usually underpinned it had been surgically removed. Celeste looked up, her eyes scanning Belle with the clinical precision of an appraiser.

She noticed the pendant immediately. Her gaze locked onto the silver moth, tracking the way the light hit its wings.

"You went somewhere," Celeste said. It wasn't a question; it was a demand for an itinerary.

"New Orleans," Belle said.

Celeste raised an eyebrow, a tiny movement that signaled a wealth of skepticism. "New Orleans. A city of ghosts and bad decisions. Which did you bring back?"

"I brought back a clearer map," Belle said. She walked toward the window, standing beside Celeste but looking out at a different horizon. "And I realized that some lessons were only half-finished."

Celeste considered her. She looked at Belle's shoulders—no longer pulled tight in a defensive hunch but settled. Still. "And?"

Belle touched the moth at her throat. The metal warmed under her thumb. "And I remembered who I was."

"Which version?" Celeste asked softly. "The girl from the gas station? Or the one I built?"

"Neither." Belle said. "The one who sets the terms."

Belle didn't flinch. She didn't move. She looked at her reflection in the glass, the New York skyline mapped out behind her like a territory waiting for a census.

Chapter 60

Belle woke before the alarm.

Not the way she had woken in the weeks after Angelique—lurching upright, the absence arriving before full consciousness, the day already wrong before it had started. This was different. Quieter. The kind of waking that happens when something has shifted in the night without announcement.

She lay still for a moment and took inventory the way Celeste had taught her to take inventory of a room—without drama, without judgment. Just information.

Angelique was still dead. That had not changed and would not change.

Betsy was still in Mississippi, still making do, still carrying damage that had not finished having its say.

Pierce was still somewhere in this city, still operating by the logic that other people's lives were resources to be managed.

None of that had changed overnight.

And yet.

She rose and stood at the mirror in the hallway. The woman looking back was no longer the girl who had arrived on a bus from

Yazoo City with purple-streaked hair and a moth tattoo she kept hidden. She was neither the version Celeste had reorganized into clean lines and deliberate silence. And she was past the woman who had stood in this same hallway after Angelique's death, unable to walk by a closed door without feeling it as an accusation.

She was something else now. Something that had not quite existed before.

She couldn't name it precisely. She wasn't sure it needed a name.

Belle touched the moth pendant where it rested against her collarbone—warm already, warmer than the room—and held it for a moment.

Then she let it go.

The city outside the window was already doing what the city did. The day was beginning whether she was ready or not.

She found, standing at the mirror in the early morning light, that she was ready.

Chapter 61

Pierce did not appear for two weeks after Angelique's death.

Belle noticed the absence only after Celeste mentioned his name.

"He asked about you," Celeste said one evening while reviewing a calendar. "I postponed."

"Why?"

"You were not calibrated."

Belle did not ask what that meant.

The next request came the following Thursday.

The Carlyle again.

Pierce was already seated when Belle entered the suite. Evening light softened the park below, the trees turning a dull amber against the approaching cold.

He stood when she entered.

"You look tired," he said.

Not accusatory. Observant.

"I'm functioning," Belle replied.

Pierce studied her for a moment before gesturing toward the chair opposite him.

"I heard about your colleague," he said.

Belle felt something tighten in her chest.

"News travels quickly," she said.

"In certain circles," Pierce replied.

He did not ask for details. He did not offer sympathy.

Instead, he poured himself a glass of water and leaned back slightly, watching her with the patient focus she had come to recognize.

"You should be careful," he said.

Belle held his gaze.

"I am."

Pierce shook his head gently.

"No," he said. "You are composed."

The distinction hung in the room.

"Celeste runs a disciplined operation," Belle said.

Pierce smiled faintly.

"Yes," he said. "Disciplined."

The way he said it made the word sound like something temporary.

For the next hour he spoke less than usual.

When he did, the conversation drifted away from markets and art and toward something more personal.

Not intimacy.

Inquiry.

"How long do you intend to stay in New York?" he asked.

"I haven't decided."

"You should."

"Why?"

Pierce leaned forward slightly.

"Because the longer you remain inside someone else's system," he said quietly, "the harder it becomes to imagine leaving it."

Belle felt the old instinct to challenge him rise in her throat.

Instead, she waited.

"You think Celeste controls me," she said.

Pierce laughed softly.

"I think Celeste understands leverage," he replied. "Which is not the same thing."

He reached for her wrist then, lightly.

Belle allowed it.

His fingers rested briefly over the moth tattoo. A gust November wind pounded the windows.

"You're wasted on most of the men she sends you to," he said.

The statement was not flirtation.

It was evaluation.

Belle did not answer.

Pierce released her wrist and leaned back again.

For the remainder of the evening, the atmosphere remained calm, almost conversational. When Belle left the suite, Pierce walked her to the door without attempting to extend the appointment.

She did not let that happen.

In the elevator, Belle watched the numbers descend.

Pierce had not crossed any lines.

But something about the conversation unsettled her more than aggression would have.

He had spoken as if Celeste's world were temporary.

As if Belle herself were something more valuable than the role she occupied.

That idea followed her all the way back to Lexington Avenue.

❧

Angelique's door remained closed down the hallway.

Outside, Manhattan moved with its usual indifferent rhythm.

She walked east toward Lexington and let the avenue absorb her. This was something she had learned without meaning to—that the city could be used this way. That if you needed to think without being watched, you walked. The movement made you invisible. Just another woman going somewhere at a pace that suggested she knew where that was.

She passed a hardware store still open at this hour; its window crowded with keys and padlocks and small tools hung on pegboard. A laundromat with two women inside folding sheets, their conversation inaudible through the glass. A restaurant closing for the night, a young man in a white apron dragging a rubber mat through the doorway, the smell of garlic and something fried reaching the sidewalk briefly before the wind took it.

This was the city Celeste had not shown her. Not the hotels or the restaurants or the avenues lined with buildings that required discretion. This was the city that ran underneath all of that—the laundromats and hardware stores and men dragging mats through doorways at eleven p.m.—the machinery that kept everything else functioning without ever being acknowledged by the people it served.

Belle had come from the machinery.

She understood it in a way the men in the suites never would.

That, she thought, was not a disadvantage.

She turned up her collar and kept walking.

❧

Betsy began calling more frequently.

At first the conversations were ordinary.

Weather.

The neighbor's dog.

A cousin Belle barely remembered getting married in Tupelo.

But something in Betsy's voice had changed.

It arrived in small hesitations.

"Billy fixed the porch steps," Betsy said during one call. "Said they were dangerous."

"That was nice of him," Belle replied carefully.

"Yeah," Betsy said. "He likes things... right."

Another time the phone rang late.

Belle answered immediately.

"You awake?" Betsy asked.

"Yes."

"I just wanted to hear your voice."

Belle waited.

In the background she heard a door close.

Heavy footsteps.

Then silence.

"How's New York?" Betsy asked too brightly.

"It's busy."

"That's good."

The conversation drifted.

Nothing explicit.

But the pauses stretched longer each time.

During the next call, Belle heard Billy's voice clearly.

Not loud.

Just present.

"Who's that?" he asked.

"My daughter," Betsy replied.

Another pause.

Then Billy again, closer now.

"Tell her hello."

Betsy laughed lightly.

"Billy says hello."

Belle stared at the apartment wall.

"How are things there?" she asked.

"Oh, fine," Betsy said quickly. "He works hard. Just gets stressed sometimes."

The word landed the way it always did.

Stressed.

Belle recognized it now as translation.

A week later Betsy called again.

Her voice sounded thinner.

"You eating enough?" she asked Belle.

"Yes."

"You sound... different."

"I am different."

Betsy laughed faintly.

"New York'll do that."

Another pause.

Then, quieter:

"He don't like when I stay on the phone too long."

Belle felt her stomach tighten.

"Who?"

"You know."

The line went silent for a moment.

Then Betsy spoke again, quickly.

"Anyway, I just wanted to check on you."

"Mom—"

But the call ended.

Belle stood in the kitchen holding the phone.

But for the first time since arriving in the city, Belle felt Mississippi reaching toward her again.

Chapter 62

The call came from Yazoo City at 6:42 a.m. Central time.

Betsy was unconscious. Blunt force trauma. Broken orbital bone. Internal bleeding. ICU.

Belle did not cry in the car to LaGuardia. She booked first class. She calculated the cost of medevac versus commercial and chose commercial.

When she entered the hospital room, Betsy did not look romantic.

The bruises were not yellowing this time.

Machines breathed rhythmically.

Belle stood at the foot of the bed and assessed the damage as if it belonged to someone else.

This is escalation, she thought. Not surprise.

The sheriff used the word domestic.

Belle used the word attempted homicide.

Billy was not present.

He had fled before the ambulance arrived.

She made three calls. An attorney. An investigator. And one more—a number she had carried from Mississippi the way you carry a scar. Not Celeste's world. Older than that.

"He won't be able to grip anything for a while," the voice said.

"Good," Belle said. Nothing more.

She hung up and stood for a moment in the hospital corridor. Celeste would have used the courts. Celeste would have said *leverage is cleaner than blood.*

Celeste had never watched her mother breathe through a machine.

Billy would get treatment eventually. County jail had its own timeline for that sort of thing. Bones healed crooked when they waited too long.

She had not made sure of anything.

She simply hadn't made sure otherwise.

Chapter 63

Betsy regained consciousness three days later.

One eye swollen shut. Speech slurred. The first thing she said was the thing Belle had been waiting for and dreading in equal measure.

"I made him mad."

Belle stood at the bedside and felt something harden in her chest that had no name she was willing to use yet.

"Stop," she said. Her voice came out quieter than she intended. "Don't you do that. Don't you dare do that."

Betsy's good eye found her.

"I just meant—"

"I know what you meant." Belle pulled the chair closer and sat. "He put you in a machine, Mama. That's on him. Not on what you said or didn't say or how the house looked or what you cooked for dinner. Him."

Betsy was quiet for a moment.

"He was always sorry after," she said.

Belle looked at her mother's hands against the white sheet. The bruising had moved into the fingers now, purple spreading toward the knuckles the way it did when the body was still accounting for damage.

"I know he was," Belle said.

She stayed until Betsy slept.

Then she went into the corridor and stood with her back against the wall and breathed until she could breathe evenly.

She called the attorney from the parking lot.

Battery. Aggravated. Possibly attempted manslaughter depending on what the DA wanted to do with the medical report. The attorney spoke in the careful sentences of a man who had learned that precision was its own form of comfort.

"He'll be charged," the attorney said. "The evidence is significant."

"Good," Belle said.

She went back inside and read Poe to her mother until visiting hours ended.

She did not look at her phone again that day.

Chapter 64

Billy was arrested two days later at his cousin's trailer outside Tupelo.

The charges were serious. The attorney confirmed them without editorializing. Aggravated battery. Flight from the scene. The medical report alone was sufficient.

Processing at the county jail was uneventful.

There had been an incident, the deputy told Belle's attorney when he called to confirm custody. Nothing serious. Inmates testing hierarchy. Billy had been transported briefly to the infirmary.

Two metacarpals fractured. Possibly three.

He would require splints. He would have difficulty gripping anything for several weeks.

Belle listened without interrupting.

"Will that affect the charges?" she asked.

"No."

"Good."

She hung up.

She sat for a moment in the plastic chair outside the ICU.

She had made three calls the morning Betsy was admitted. The attorney. The investigator. And the third one—the number she had carried from Mississippi the way you carry a scar. Not Celeste's world. Older than that. A favor called in from a place she had told herself she had left behind.

Celeste would have said leverage is cleaner than blood.

Celeste had never watched her mother breathe through a machine.

The law would take Billy apart slowly, efficiently, the way the law did. The charges were real. The evidence was significant. He would not walk away from this.

The broken fingers were separate from the charges.

Belle had made sure of that.

She hadn't made sure of the promptness.

In the ICU, Betsy's hands lay limp against the white sheets. Purple fading toward yellow.

Belle looked at them for a long time.

Chapter 65

Back in New York, Belle resumed her bookings at an increased rate.

Clients sensed something altered. She would not name it.

She no longer waited for approval.

She no longer looked at doors as exits.

Halbrecht called Celeste that week regarding irregular exposure connected to a partner's private habits.

Celeste listened.

Belle listened from the hallway outside the office.

Men with power feared embarrassment more than death.

Angelique had died because of miscalculation.

Belle had learned the difference between accident and intention.

She preferred intention.

Chapter 66

New York felt louder after Mississippi.

Not physically. The traffic still moved with the same mechanical rhythm along Lexington. The elevators still opened and closed with patient precision. The doorman still nodded without curiosity.

But Belle heard something else beneath it now.

Velocity.

The city moved forward without hesitation, without reflection. Mississippi had weight. New York had momentum.

She had returned three days earlier.

The hospital smell still clung to her memory: antiseptic, plastic tubing, the quiet machinery around Betsy's bed. Her mother's face looked smaller against the white pillow, the bruising already shifting from purple toward yellow.

Billy had not been there.

The sheriff had spoken in careful sentences.

Domestic disturbance.

No arrest yet.

Belle had stayed a week in Yazoo City.

❧

Long enough to see Betsy awake. Long enough to hear her insist it had been a misunderstanding. Long enough to recognize the familiar shape of denial rebuilding itself around the damage.

The following morning Belle had left.

Celeste's car met her at LaGuardia.

Celeste had not asked many questions.

"Is everything alright?" Celeste said.

"Yes."

"Then the situation is stable."

Belle had nodded.

Structure had resumed immediately.

Appointments rescheduled.

Calendar adjusted.

Life re-entering its narrow rails.

❧

She had not cried in Yazoo City.

She had not cried on the plane back. She had sat in 2C with a glass of water she didn't drink and watched the cloud cover break apart over New Jersey and felt the two versions of herself sorting back into their correct positions—Annabelle, who had stood in a hospital corridor at six in the morning calculating the cost of medevac, and Belle, who had a Pierce appointment on Thursday and a wardrobe that did not include anything she had packed for Mississippi.

The cab from LaGuardia had taken the Triborough bridge. She had watched the city assemble itself through the window the way she had watched it the first time from the plane—grids, steel, compression—except this time she knew what was inside it. The particular cold of the Carlyle's upper floors. The way Pierce watched her from across a room. The weight of Angelique's shoes by a door that didn't open anymore.

She had set her bag down inside the apartment and stood in the hallway for a long time.

The apartment smelled the same.

That was the thing that surprised her. She had half-expected it to smell of Mississippi—of cut grass and old heat and the particular staleness of rooms where things had gone wrong—the way you sometimes carried a place back inside you without meaning to.

But the apartment smelled of filtered air and Angelique's jasmine, faint now, fainter each week, and the specific neutrality of a space that had been designed to contain rather than comfort.

Belle had breathed it in once.

Then she had unpacked.

Now she stood in front of the mirror in the apartment hallway adjusting the sleeve of her jacket. Angelique's room remained empty. Celeste had still not reassigned it.

Belle sometimes wondered if that was deliberate.

Angelique had been gone for weeks now, yet the space she left behind continued shaping the apartment like a missing wall.

Her phone vibrated on the table.

A message from Celeste.

Pierce. 7:30. Carlyle.

Belle stared at the screen for a moment longer than necessary.

Then she picked up her coat.

Pierce stood at the window when she entered the suite.

The park beyond the glass was dark now, the trees bare enough that the city lights filtered through them in broken lines.

Pierce was speaking about a property acquisition in London when he said, without transition:

"How is your mother?"

Belle's stillness shifted—barely, but it shifted.

"Fine," she said.

Pierce continued as if the question had been ordinary. "Yazoo City, Mississippi. Still in the same place, I believe. The trailer on County Road 102." He lifted his glass. "Billy Johnson is no longer in the picture, I understand. That must be a relief."

The room did not change. Same curtains, same light, same city beyond the glass. But something in its proportions shifted—as if the space between Belle and the door had quietly lengthened without anything physically moving.

"You've had someone watching my family," she said.

Pierce neither confirmed nor denied it.

"I like to understand the architecture of things," he said. "The people a person protects tell you more about them than the people they choose." He set his glass down. "You wired money the day after she was admitted. You booked a same-day flight. You were back in New York within the week." He paused. "That's not sentiment. That's discipline under pressure. Most people can't manage it."

"That's a significant overstep," Belle said.

"Is it?" His expression was genuinely curious—the look of a man who had considered the question carefully and arrived at a different answer. "You are, by any reasonable measure, the most capable person in Celeste's operation. You've been functioning inside a system designed for women with far fewer options than you have." He paused. "I'm trying to understand what you want."

"You could have asked."

"I did ask." He tilted his head slightly. "You give Celeste's answers. I wanted yours."

Belle held his gaze.

He had not found Betsy through Celeste. Celeste didn't know about the wired money, the flight, the hospital room, Billy's name. Belle had kept that world completely separate. It was the one thing she had kept completely separate.

"She's recovering," Belle said. Her voice was even.

"I'm glad," Pierce said, and he sounded as though he meant it. That was the part that required the most careful management—the fact that he did not seem cruel. He seemed *thorough*.

"I'd like to go," she said.

Pierce stood immediately. Walked her to the door. Held it.

"Of course," he said pleasantly.

In the elevator, Belle stared at the numbers descending.

He had not raised his voice. He had not touched her. He had simply demonstrated that he knew her mother's address and her mother's bruises and the name of the man who had put them there.

And he had offered it the way you offer someone a gift—as proof that you have been paying attention.

As proof that you have been paying attention *for a long time.*

The lobby arrived. Belle walked through it without checking her reflection.

She was already calculating.

Not whether Pierce was dangerous.

She knew that now.

She was calculating how long he had been watching before she had any reason to watch back.

❧

Outside, the rain had arrived.

Not the way storms arrived in Mississippi—announced by wind, preceded by the particular green light that meant take cover, arriving with intention. This was New York rain. It simply appeared, the way the city produced most things—without ceremony, as if it had always been there and you had only just noticed.

Belle stood under the building's narrow overhang for a moment.

The street had gone dark and reflective, headlights smearing across the wet pavement in long orange strokes. A cab moved through the intersection without slowing. A man in a good coat walked past holding a briefcase over his head, which accomplished nothing and which he seemed to know.

She stepped out into it.

The rain was cold and specific, the kind that found the gap between your collar and your neck and stayed there. She did not walk faster. She had learned that from Celeste—the weather was not a reason to hurry; hurrying in the rain only told the city you were surprised by it, and the city noticed everything.

She walked.

The pendant was cool against her collarbone and then warm. The rain ran down the back of her neck and she let it. Around her Manhattan absorbed the storm the way it absorbed everything—without adjustment, without complaint, simply continuing.

By the time she reached Lexington her coat was wet through.

She did not mind.

There was something clarifying about being rained on in a city that didn't care. No shelter being offered. No one checking if she was alright. Just the rain doing what rain did and Belle doing what Belle did and the city indifferent to both.

She walked another block before flagging a cab.

Inside, the windows fogged immediately.

She watched the city blur behind the glass and felt, for the first time since entering that apartment, that she was breathing at her own pace. The storm continued without her.

Chapter 67

Thomas Halbrecht preferred numbers because numbers did not perform.

Men performed. Markets performed. Even truth performed when it passed through enough hands. But numbers, when arranged correctly, had a way of settling into place like weight on a scale.

The Easton Agency payments he had already accounted for. A retainer. Discreet. The kind of arrangement men in Pierce's position maintained without particular creativity. Halbrecht had no interest in Pierce's private habits—only in whether they created exposure for the firm. Celeste Voss ran a disciplined operation. He had satisfied himself of that.

It was the other transfers that bothered him.

Identical amounts. Identical spacing. Thirty days apart, each landing inside the same seventy-two-hour window.

Predictability was not Daniel Pierce's style.

Pierce was cautious in the visible places. He varied restaurants. Rotated hotels. Paid for discretion the way other men paid for comfort. Halbrecht had known him long enough to understand the difference between indulgence and exposure.

This was neither.

This was framing.

The conference room overlooking Park Avenue was empty when the investigators arrived. Halbrecht preferred it that way. No assistants. No files on the table except the single folder he had brought with him.

The older of the two men sat first. The other remained standing a moment longer, as if confirming the room contained no surprises.

"Mr. Halbrecht," the older one said.

Halbrecht inclined his head slightly.

"What do you have."

The man opened a tablet rather than a folder.

"Mr. Pierce's pattern has changed," he said. "For the first eight months we observed multiple meetings. Different women. Different agencies. Hotels varied. Frequency irregular." He slid the tablet across the table. "That stopped."

A series of still images appeared—hotel lobbies, elevator banks, sidewalks outside buildings Halbrecht recognized by reputation even if he had never entered them. In each frame Pierce appeared. And in each frame, a woman arrived separately. Young. Composed. Dark hair. The same woman.

"One individual," the investigator said. "Weekly. Sometimes more."

Halbrecht studied the photograph.

Not the woman's face.

Her posture.

She walked into the elevator without looking around.

That interested him.

"Do we have identification."

"Not yet. She arrives independently and leaves independently. No shared registration."

"The money."

The younger investigator spoke.

"He's routing personal funds through a Delaware LLC. Linebridge Capital. Single owner, nominee filing, formed three years ago. The structure resembles payment clearing—identical transfers, each followed by smaller outgoing payments within twenty-four hours. Rounded amounts. No invoices."

"To whom."

"Several entities. Standard merchant processors, and two connected to offshore wagering platforms."

The room went quiet.

Pierce was reckless in private, but he was not stupid. If his name was attached to money moving through gambling channels—personal funds or not—that was not merely embarrassing.

That was regulatory.

"Hedging?" Halbrecht asked.

"The structure is consistent with it. We're still tracing."

Halbrecht closed the tablet.

"Continue the trace. And identify the woman."

The investigators stood. At the door the older man paused.

"His movements have tightened. He's favoring two properties—the Lowell and the Mark. She arrives alone each time. Leaves alone."

Halbrecht nodded once.

The door closed behind them.

Park Avenue moved below the window like a quiet machine. Cars sliding through intersections. Men in dark coats walking with purpose.

Halbrecht reopened the photograph.

Not her face. Her posture. She walked into the elevator without looking around. No fear. No recklessness. Simply arriving.

Pierce had not simply found someone.

He had selected her.

Halbrecht closed the tablet.

Predictability. Structure. One woman. Every week. And a clearing company moving money into places where money rarely returned the same shape it entered.

Daniel Pierce was building something.

Or losing control of something.

Halbrecht had not decided which yet.

He turned back to the window and watched Park Avenue move beneath him, numbers arranging themselves in his mind the way they always did.

Eventually, everything reduced to pattern.

And patterns always broke somewhere.

He intended to be standing nearby when this one did.

Chapter 68

The restaurant was quiet in the expensive way quiet places are.

Belle sat across from Charles Whitaker, a polite man in his early sixties who spoke mostly about his grandchildren and the view from his Connecticut house. He had ordered wine she did not drink and a steak she barely touched.

He was kind. Forgettable. The sort of client Celeste preferred.

Halfway through dessert, Belle excused herself.

"Ladies' room," she said with a small smile.

Whitaker nodded. "Take your time."

The hallway was narrow and softly lit, carpet swallowing the sound of her heels. The restroom door was heavy, polished brass handle worn smooth.

Inside, the room was empty.

Belle washed her hands slowly, studying herself in the mirror the way she had learned to do before returning to a table—checking the details: lipstick, posture, expression.

The door behind her opened.

She assumed another woman had entered.

The man in the mirror told her otherwise.

He moved fast.

A cloth pressed hard against her mouth and nose.

The smell was sharp and chemical.

Belle tried to twist away, elbow striking air, but a second hand locked around her wrists with practiced strength. The counter struck her hip.

The mirror fractured into light.

Her legs stopped belonging to her.

The last thing she saw before the floor rose up was the man lowering her carefully, almost professionally, to the tile.

☙

Whitaker waited ten minutes.

Then fifteen.

He checked his watch.

Another five minutes passed before he asked the hostess if someone might check the ladies' room.

The hostess returned a moment later.

"It's empty, sir."

Whitaker frowned.

"Strange," he said. "She said she'd be right back."

☙

Celeste answered on the second ring.

"Celeste Voss."

"Good evening," Whitaker said politely. "This is Charles Whitaker. I'm afraid your associate appears to have left."

Celeste's tone did not change.

"Left?"

"Yes. She excused herself and never returned. I assumed perhaps she received another engagement."

Celeste paused.

“That would be unlike her, Mr. Whitaker.”

“Well,” he said awkwardly, “I thought you should know.”

“Thank you,” Celeste replied.

She hung up and immediately dialed Belle’s phone.

Straight to voicemail.

Celeste tried again.

Then once more.

Her expression did not change, but something behind her eyes hardened.

Belle Devereaux did not walk out on clients.

Chapter 69

Crystal chandeliers and quiet money.

The charity gala filled the ballroom of the Pierre with the careful laughter of people who expected to be photographed. Massive chandeliers threw light across a ceiling of silver and gold leaf, and the colonnaded walls gave the room the feeling of a place that had been built to remind you of your own scale—that you were a guest here, however well you were dressed, however carefully you had arrived.

Thomas Halbrecht stood near the bar beside his partner.

Daniel Pierce looked immaculate in black tie, his posture relaxed, his smile practiced.

"You should pretend to enjoy this," Halbrecht said.

"I am enjoying it."

"You look like a man attending his own audit."

Pierce smiled faintly.

"Charity functions are audits."

Halbrecht lifted his glass.

"True."

Pierce's phone buzzed.

He glanced at his phone but did not answer.

Halbrecht noticed.

"Problem?"

"Agency business," Pierce said lightly.

He slipped the phone back into his pocket.

Across the ballroom a string quartet played something tasteful and forgettable.

Halbrecht's phone rang.

He looked at the screen and raised an eyebrow.

"Interesting."

"Who is it?" Pierce asked.

"Celeste Voss."

Pierce did not react.

Halbrecht answered.

"Celeste."

Her voice was controlled.

"I'm looking for Pierce."

Halbrecht looked directly at the man beside him.

"He's standing next to me," Halbrecht said calmly.

Celeste was silent for a moment.

"I see."

"Is there a problem?"

"One of my women has disappeared."

Halbrecht's gaze remained on Pierce.

"Disappeared."

"Yes."

A long pause followed.

"Well," Halbrecht said mildly, "Pierce has been with me all evening."

Pierce lifted his glass and gave the faintest shrug.

Halbrecht ended the call.

Neither man spoke for several seconds.

"How do you know Celeste?" Pierce asked.

"Everyone in this city knows Celeste," he said, finally adding, "You really should stop doing things that cause women to disappear."

Pierce smiled.

"I haven't the faintest idea what you mean."

Halbrecht studied him.

"Of course you don't."

Across the ballroom, the orchestra began another piece.

Halbrecht finished his drink.

❧

She woke slowly, the way one rises from under deep water.

The chemical sweetness still coated the back of her throat. Her head felt heavy but intact. She kept her eyes closed for a long moment and listened to her own breathing—steady, even, controlled. The way Celeste had taught her. The way she had once kept it steady behind the counter at Phil's when trouble walked through the door.

When she finally opened her eyes, the room came into focus. Clean. Impersonal. Staged. A wide window showing a gray slice of the Hudson. In the upper corner, a small black camera watched with mechanical patience.

Belle lay still. She did not panic. Panic was wasteful.

She took inventory: one visible door with a digital keypad, furniture too heavy to be useful, no immediate weapons. No restraints. She flexed her fingers slowly. Nothing broken.

Mississippi still lived in her, quiet but present. It had taught her how to sit inside ugly situations and wait for the shape of them to reveal itself.

She sat up slowly, spine straight even though no one had told her to. The camera was recording. She knew that. Let it record.

She thought of her mother. She thought of Angelique's closed door. She thought of the legal pad she would need and the long game she might have to play.

Then she folded those thoughts away with careful discipline.

When Pierce finally arrived carrying two paper cups of coffee, she was sitting on the edge of the bed with her hands resting quietly in her lap. Her posture was perfect. Her eyes were clear.

He set one cup on the low table between them and sat down opposite her, studying her the way a man studies a problem he intends to solve.

"You understand the situation," he said.

Belle met his gaze without flinching.

"I understand you've taken me," she replied. Her voice was calm, almost polite.

Inside, something older and harder than anything Celeste had taught her clicked into place.

She would survive this.

And she would do it on her own terms.

Chapter 70

Celeste stood at the window of her townhouse looking down at Seventy-Sixth Street.

Four days.

The client, Charles Whitaker, had called with polite confusion. Belle had excused herself to the ladies' room during dinner at the restaurant and never returned. No note. No message. Nothing.

Celeste had already spoken to the maître d', to the hotel staff, to the few drivers who might have seen anything. The trail was clean. Too clean.

She tried Belle's number again. Straight to voicemail.

She set the phone down on the marble console with deliberate care. She did not allow herself to pace. She did not allow the cold knot in her chest to tighten into fear. Not yet.

Belle Devereaux did not disappear.

Celeste had built this life on control, on predictability, on understanding exactly what men like Pierce were capable of. She had known the risk the moment Halbrecht first mentioned his partner's private habits. She had still sent Belle to him.

Now the apartment on Seventy-Fifth felt too quiet. Angelique's door remained closed at the end of the hall. The kitchen still held the faint trace of jasmine that would not fade.

Celeste turned away from the window.

She would not call the police. Not yet. That would open everything—the clients, the contracts, the other women. Pierce knew that. He was counting on it.

She picked up the phone and dialed a different number.

"Mr. Halbrecht," she said when he answered. "We have a problem."

Chapter 71

For the first twelve days Belle worked the keypad with quiet, methodical discipline.

She had seen the first number—upper left corner, almost certainly a 4. That single digit changed everything. It reduced ten thousand possibilities to one thousand. But Pierce could never know she had seen it.

So on the legal pad she started writing numbers in the 9000s.

She marked each failed attempt with a neat vertical line, page after page of them. If he ever looked—and she was certain the camera would show him eventually—he would see a woman still grinding through the full ten thousand combinations like a fool. Not a woman who had already narrowed the field.

Alone in the long hours between his visits, she sat at the kitchen counter and continued the real work in her head while feeding the pad the decoy numbers. The repetition steadied her. It gave her mind something to hold onto while the rest of her adjusted to the cage.

She still told herself this might only be leverage. Extreme, ugly leverage. She was not yet ready to believe he would kill her.

But the possibility lived in the room with her now, quiet and patient as the camera in the corner.

She turned another page on the legal pad and wrote 9127.

Then 9128.

Then 9129.

She marked the failure with a clean line and began the next set.

Chapter 72

Halbrecht was already seated when Celeste arrived at the small restaurant in the Village. He had chosen a table in the back corner, far from the windows and other diners.

Celeste sat down without removing her coat. She ordered water. Halbrecht waited until the waiter had disappeared before he spoke.

"We've confirmed the building," he said. "West side. Heavy renovation. Pierce has been visiting nearly every day for weeks. We believe she is on the fourth or fifth floor."

Celeste's hands remained folded on the table. She said nothing.

Halbrecht continued, his voice low and measured.

"My people have been watching discreetly. Construction noise covers a great deal. But we are close. The question now is what we do when we find her."

He let the silence sit between them. Celeste studied him the way she studied difficult clients—looking past the surface to the architecture beneath.

Halbrecht leaned forward slightly.

"From the firm's perspective," he said, "it may be cleaner if she is never found. Permanently. The liability is enormous. The clients.

The financial trails. The other women who might decide to talk if this becomes public. Everything we have built could come apart."

Celeste did not flinch. She had expected this.

"I would rather find her myself," she said quietly. "I can manage her. I can contain the damage. But if the police reach her first, or if she decides to speak freely, we lose control of the entire situation."

Halbrecht's expression did not change, but his eyes hardened.

"I am not suggesting we do nothing," he said. "I am suggesting we be realistic about the risks. If Pierce has already decided she is a liability that cannot be managed, then keeping her alive may cost more than either of us is willing to pay. I will do what is necessary to protect the firm. That includes making sure this situation does not explode in a way that destroys everything we have spent decades building."

The threat was quiet, but unmistakable.

Celeste met his gaze.

"Pierce needs to understand the expense," she said. "Not just the financial expense. The personal one. He has grown careless. Arrogant. If he believes he can burn my operation to cover his mistakes, he should be reminded that fire spreads in both directions."

Halbrecht studied her for a long moment.

"You still think you can control her?"

"I know I can," Celeste said. "Better than he can. Better than the police can. She is one of mine. That still means something."

Halbrecht leaned back in his chair. The silence stretched.

"Very well," he said finally. "We find her. We extract her. And then you handle her. But if at any point it becomes clear that she cannot be contained..."

He left the rest unsaid.

Celeste nodded once.

"I understand," she said.

Chapter 73

Mei arrived at Celeste's townhouse without calling first.

She did not wait to be invited inside. She stepped past Celeste into the sitting room, her movements precise and unhurried.

"Six weeks," Mei said. Her voice was quiet, but it carried.

Celeste closed the door. She did not offer tea or a seat.

"I know how long it's been," she replied.

Mei turned to face her. Her eyes were completely still.

"You knew it was Pierce from the beginning."

"I suspected."

"Same thing," Mei said. The words landed flat.

Celeste studied the younger woman.

"We are watching the building," Celeste said. "Halbrecht's people are close. If we move too soon and he feels us, he will kill her before we can reach the unit."

Mei did not blink.

"And if we wait too long?"

Celeste's expression did not change, but something behind her eyes tightened.

“Then we lose her anyway.”

The silence stretched.

Mei took one step closer.

“You built this,” she said softly. “You brought her into it. And now you are calculating whether it is worth losing her to protect it.”

Celeste did not look away.

“I am calculating how to keep her alive,” she said.

Mei held her gaze for a long moment—the same full, quiet inventory she brought to every room.

“Then calculate faster,” she said.

She turned and walked out without another word.

Celeste stood alone in the sitting room for a long time after the door closed.

Chapter 74

On the eighteenth night Pierce stayed longer than usual.

He brought wine and poured a glass for her without asking. Belle accepted it but barely drank.

He spoke for a long time about leverage. About problems that had to be handled permanently. About men who became liabilities and how those liabilities sometimes simply ceased to exist. He did not use the word "kill," but the shape of it was unmistakable now.

Belle listened with perfect stillness. She let her face show quiet understanding. She asked a soft question at the right moment. She let him see what looked like the slow dawning of alignment.

Later, when the door closed behind him and the apartment returned to its sterile silence, Belle sat on the floor with her back against the wall.

She pressed two fingers hard against the moth pendant until the metal bit into her skin.

He would kill her.

She understood that now with complete and terrible clarity.

For thirty minutes she allowed herself to feel the full weight of it. Then she stood up, washed her face with cold water, and returned to the kitchen counter.

She opened the legal pad to a fresh page and wrote another set of numbers in the 9000s.

She marked the failures with the same neat vertical lines.

She was still working both games at once.

Chapter 75

Belle found the book late one afternoon while Pierce was gone.

In the bottom drawer of the narrow dresser, beneath a folded blanket, she saw it: her own copy of *Lord Jim*. The spine was worn exactly where she had worn it. Inside the front cover was the inscription in Jonathan's careful hand.

And beside it, her hairbrush. The one with the tortoiseshell handle. A few strands of her own dark hair still caught in the bristles.

She stood very still, holding the brush.

He had been in her apartment. He had gone through her things. He had chosen these specific objects and brought them here like offerings.

The invasion was so complete, so casual, that for a moment the room tilted.

She closed the drawer slowly. When she turned back to the legal pad, her hand was steady.

Later that evening, when Pierce arrived, Belle was sitting at the kitchen counter with *Lord Jim* open in front of her.

"You brought my book," she said quietly. "And my hairbrush."

Pierce paused near the island, watching her reaction.

"I thought you might want something familiar," he said.

Belle touched the spine of the book with one finger.

"That was... thoughtful," she said. Her voice caught just enough to sound real. "I didn't expect that."

She met his eyes.

"I'm tired of fighting, Daniel. I'm tired of being small."

She let the silence sit between them, heavy and deliberate.

Pierce studied her for a long moment. Something in his posture eased.

"You're starting to understand," he said.

Chapter 76

Leila stood in the middle of Celeste's kitchen at a quarter past two in the morning, coat still on.

"Six weeks," she said. "Six fucking weeks, Celeste."

Celeste remained at the counter, hands wrapped around a mug of tea that had gone cold.

Mei sat at the table, silent.

Halbrecht had called earlier. His people were almost certain they had the floor. But Pierce had not left the building in thirty-six hours.

Celeste looked at the two women.

"If we force this now," she said quietly, "he will kill her before they can reach the unit."

Leila's laugh was sharp and ugly. "So we just sit here while he decides whether she's useful enough to keep breathing?"

Celeste met her eyes.

"Yes," she said. "That is exactly what we do."

Chapter 77

By the end of the fifth week Pierce had begun to relax in her presence.

He spoke as if she were already part of his future. He brought her the exact brand of tea she kept in her apartment. He told her more about the offshore accounts, about how certain liabilities would simply cease to exist.

Belle listened with the softness she had spent weeks perfecting. She asked intelligent questions. She let him see what looked like genuine alignment.

Alone afterward, she sat at the kitchen counter holding the hairbrush he had brought her. A few of her own dark strands were still caught in the bristles.

The violation was so complete it almost felt intimate.

She placed the brush back in the drawer and returned to the legal pad.

She wrote another set of numbers in the 9000s.

She marked the failures with the same neat vertical lines.

She was becoming very good at being the woman he wanted her to be.

Chapter 78

On the thirty-fourth night Pierce said, "We're going out."

Belle looked up from the book in her lap.

"A dinner. Two floors down. Another unit in the building. There will be staff. Cameras. Real eyes." He studied her. "I need to see how you behave when there are other people around."

She nodded slowly.

"I understand," she said.

She dressed carefully. She brushed her hair with the tortoiseshell brush he had brought her. When she looked in the mirror, the woman staring back was composed, elegant, believable.

The dinner was a test. Belle performed with everything she had learned.

She spoke about the future as though she had already chosen it. She offered one small, useful refinement to something Pierce said. She let her hand rest near his once. She smiled at the right moments with the exact warmth that would read as budding loyalty.

As Belle set her napkin on the table the waiter stepped forward to pull back her chair. His hand brushed the edge of her plate. She thanked him with the small, automatic courtesy of a woman who had learned to acknowledge staff without acknowledging them.

She had pressed the folded note into his palm when Pierce turned to reach for his jacket.

The waiter did not look at it. He did not look at her.

Good.

When they returned to the apartment and the door closed behind them, Pierce lingered in the entryway.

"You did well tonight," he said.

Belle met his gaze and let a small, tired smile touch her lips.

"I'm tired of fighting what's inevitable," she replied softly.

Chapter 79

On the thirty-seventh day a knock came at the door.

Sharp. Official. Twice.

Belle froze at the kitchen counter, legal pad open in front of her. Her heart slammed against her ribs.

She knew Pierce was beginning to trust her. Answering this knock could destroy everything.

She stayed perfectly still. The knock came again. A male voice called something muffled about maintenance.

Belle did not move. She did not breathe loudly. She stared at the door like it was a loaded gun.

The knocking stopped.

Footsteps moved away.

Belle let out a long, silent breath, closed her eyes for three seconds, then turned the page on the legal pad and wrote another set of numbers in the 9000s.

She marked the failure with a clean line.

She was still choosing.

Chapter 80

She was losing her mind.

Not loudly. Not in ways Pierce would see. But quietly, in the small hours, in the spaces between numbers on the legal pad, in the long silences after he left.

Six weeks.

Six weeks of smiling when she wanted to scream. Six weeks of saying "I understand" when she wanted to drive something sharp into his throat. Six weeks of performing a softer, more compliant version of herself so convincingly that she sometimes forgot where the performance ended and the real Belle began.

She sat on the floor with her back against the wall, knees drawn up, arms wrapped tightly around them. The legal pad lay beside her, covered in thousands of crossed-out numbers.

She was so tired.

Tired of calculating every word, every gesture, every micro-expression. Tired of pretending she was becoming what he wanted when every cell in her body raged against the cage.

Mississippi whispered to her at night. The old Annabelle wanted blood. The refined Belle demanded precision and patience.

Both of them were right.

Both of them were dangerous.

She pressed her forehead against her knees and breathed through her teeth until the worst of the storm passed. She did not fight the madness. She simply endured it.

When it thinned, she turned to the back page of the legal pad. Forty marks. Neat rows of five.

She had not missed a day.

She stood up, washed her face with cold water, and returned to the legal pad.

She wrote another set of numbers in the 9000s.

She marked the failure with a clean line.

Then she whispered, so softly the camera could not possibly hear:

"I am still here. I am still choosing."

Chapter 81

They left the building on the forty-second morning.

Before they stepped out of the apartment, Pierce had paused at the marble console. Belle's purse sat there on a silver tray, her phone beside it, plugged in and fully charged. He had picked it up, checked the screen, then set it back down.

"Yours," he had said.

Now, as they walked through the marble lobby, Belle carried that purse.

At the center of the lobby she stopped.

She turned to face him.

"Daniel," she said. Her voice was low, almost gentle.

He looked at her, expectant. Pleased.

"I've been keeping notes," she said calmly. "Every day. Contemporaneous memoranda. Everything you said. Every detail about how you would kill me if I did not fully commit. Every account number. Every name. Every plan for the new structure. Copies have already been delivered to people who can act on them. If anything happens to me, or to my mother, they become public immediately."

Pierce's expression did not change at first.

"You're bluffing," he said quietly.

Belle met his gaze without hesitation.

"No. During the dinner two floors down—the night you tested me—I passed the first set of notes to the waiter. Along with instructions and a phone number. I told him it was a private legal matter and that his discretion would be rewarded. He did it. I watched him pocket the envelope."

The stillness that moved across his face was small, but she saw it.

"You taught me how to wait," she continued. "You taught me how to become exactly what someone needs me to be. How to sit inside someone else's design for forty-two days until the moment it could be turned against them."

She took one clean step backward.

"I'm finished with your design."

She turned and walked toward the entrance with the same measured gait she had practiced for years. No rush. No fear in her body.

"Town car, please," she told the doorman.

She did not look back.

When the car door closed behind her and the vehicle pulled smoothly into traffic, Belle sat very straight. She pressed two fingers to the moth pendant at her throat and held them there until the metal grew warm against her skin.

She had not escaped.

She had dismantled him from the inside.

And she had done it without ever raising her voice.

Chapter 82

Belle sat in the back of the town car and took a breath—several breaths.

Her phone showed hundreds of missed calls and unread messages—the screen was a scroll of red notification badges that refused to end.

She scrolled through them without expression. Celeste. Celeste. Mei. Celeste. A number she didn't recognize twice. Leila.

Betsy. Betsy. Betsy. Betsy.

Eleven times.

Belle rode in silence for a moment, the traffic moving with its usual indifference. Then she called her mother.

Betsy answered on the first ring.

"Where in the hell have you been." Not a question. The voice of a woman who had been frightened long enough that the fear had curdled into anger, which was how Betsy always processed things she couldn't afford to feel directly.

"I'm fine," Belle said.

"That is not what I asked."

"I know."

A pause. The television in the background. Always the television.

"Two months," Betsy said, quieter now. "I called the number you left me. Some man answered and said he didn't know anyone by that name."

"I'll explain later."

"You'll explain now."

Belle almost smiled. "I was unavoidably detained."

Betsy was silent for a moment. Then: "That man."

"It's handled."

Another silence. Longer.

"You sound different," Betsy said.

"I'm fine, Mama."

"I didn't ask if you were fine. I said you sound different."

Belle leaned against the leather seat. Above her Manhattan continued its business, glass and steel and the distant percussion of a city that did not pause for private emergencies.

"I've been thinking," Belle said.

"About."

"You."

Betsy laughed once, dry and short. "Now I know something happened. You only think about me when something happens."

That landed close enough to true that Belle let it pass.

"Where are you living," Belle said.

"Same place."

"Still with Billy's things in it."

Betsy was quiet.

"Mama."

"I threw most of it out," Betsy said. A defense dressed as information.

Belle closed her eyes briefly. The same trailer. The same rooms. The same walls that had held Billy's belt and Billy's boots and Billy's particular idea of what a woman owed him.

"I want you somewhere else," Belle said.

"Annabelle—"

"I want you somewhere with a yard. Somewhere quiet." She paused. "Somewhere with someone to look after you properly."

"I don't need looking after."

"I know you don't." Belle kept her voice even. "I need you looked after. There's a difference."

Betsy made a sound that wasn't quite agreement and wasn't quite refusal.

"I'm not going to a home," she said.

"Not a home. A house—a real one. With a woman who will cook and keep you company and make sure you're not alone at two in the morning when the edges start cutting."

Silence.

"How do you know about the two in the morning," Betsy said softly.

Belle didn't answer that.

"I'm going to make some calls," Belle said. "I'll handle the money. You don't need to worry about any of that."

"Annabelle—"

"Mama."

A long pause.

"She better not be preachy," Betsy finally said.

Belle felt something loosen in her chest that had been tight for longer than two months. For years, maybe.

"I'll specify that," she said.

"And I want a porch."

"You'll have a porch."

"With a ceiling fan. The humidity is bad in August."

"I know it is."

Another pause. When Betsy spoke again her voice was smaller, stripped of its defensive architecture.

"You're sure you're alright," she said.

"Yes."

"Because you can come home. If you need to."

Belle looked up at the buildings rising around her, the compressed sky between them, the city that had made her into something Mississippi never could have.

"I know," she said. "I don't need to."

"Okay," Betsy said. Quietly. "Okay."

She hung up.

Belle rode quietly for a moment.

Then something moved through her that she hadn't felt in forty-two days—not grief, not relief, something with less name than either—her hand shook as she found the button on the armrest, and the privacy screen rose between her and the driver with a soft mechanical sound.

She pressed two fingers to her mouth.

It came the way it always came when you had held something too long—not loudly, not all at once. Just the first small sound, and then the next, and then she bent forward and let it happen because there was no camera here and no legal pad and no version of herself that needed to be maintained for anyone.

The city moved past the windows. The driver drove.

She breathed through it until it was done, then sat up—straight. Wiped her face with the heel of her hand. Pressed two fingers to the moth pendant until the metal bit into her skin.

She lowered the screen.

She made four more calls.

By evening, she had a name, two references checked, and a three-bedroom house outside Yazoo City with a porch facing west and a ceiling fan that worked.

She did not go back to Mississippi.

She didn't need to.

Then she called Celeste.

Chapter 83

Belle sat on the edge of the bed, phone in her hand, her breathing shallow and careful. The apartment felt too still.

The door eased open. Leila slipped in, her expression wary but kind.

"You want company?"

Belle shook her head, but didn't say "no." Leila sat nearby, leaving space.

Silence. Belle stared at her hands.

"It was just... quiet," she said, her voice low and strained. "The whole time. He said it was a test, or a favor, or—" She shook her head. "I kept thinking I'd done something wrong, but he just wanted me to wait. To see if I'd break."

Leila's voice was steady. "You didn't."

Belle gave a brief, brittle laugh. "I don't know. Maybe I did a little."

Leila reached over, her hand resting lightly on the bed between them—a gesture of solidarity, not comfort.

Belle looked at her, eyes tired. "Sometimes I could hear people in the hallway. Someone even knocked, but I didn't know if it was one of his tests. I kept thinking, if I scream, does anyone care? But I didn't. I just waited. I did what I was supposed to."

Leila's reply was quiet but firm. "You're not supposed to be locked up. You know that, right?"

Belle nodded once. "I know."

She sat still long enough that the silence stopped waiting for her to fill it.

Chapter 84

They filled the room quickly.

Six of them. Some still wearing coats. One with her phone in her hand as if she had come directly from another appointment.

Every face turned toward Belle first.

"You're back," one of them said.

Belle nodded.

No one asked what happened.

They could see enough.

Then the room shifted.

All eyes moved to Celeste.

"You didn't call the police," one woman said.

Celeste stood at the head of the table like a judge hearing a case she had already decided.

"No."

"You knew who took her."

"I suspected."

"Same difference."

Celeste's voice remained calm.

"If Pierce had been publicly investigated, every client connected to this agency would have been exposed."

"Good," someone snapped.

"Not good," Celeste said quietly. "Catastrophic."

Silence spread across the room.

"You chose the business," another girl said.

"I chose survival."

No one answered that.

The silence that followed was its own verdict.

Sofia was the first to stand. She did it without announcement, the way she did most things---a calculation completed, a decision implemented. She picked up her bag and walked to the door without looking back. No anger. No performance. Simply a woman who had already moved on before she left the room.

The other three followed close behind her. No words between them. Just coats lifted, bags collected, the quiet choreography of women who had already decided before they arrived.

Mei rose a moment later. She crossed toward the door with the same still attention she brought to everything. At the threshold she stopped and turned. She looked at Celeste the way she looked at men in restaurants---a full, quiet inventory that missed nothing and forgave nothing. She held it for one beat. Then she walked out.

The door did not close behind her.

Leila was still in her chair.

She took her time. Put on her coat. Straightened the collar. Picked up her bag and settled it on her shoulder with the particular deliberateness of a woman who wanted every movement to be understood. Then she turned to Celeste.

"I can't believe you thought this place was worth more than Belle."

She walked out.

The door closed.

Celeste did not speak.

There was nothing to say. Leila had not left a space for response. The statement wasn't an accusation waiting for a defense. It was a fact, delivered and filed, the way Leila had always delivered things that mattered.

When the door closed, only three things remained.

Celeste.

Belle.

And the silence of a business that had just lost its elite workforce.

Celeste stood very still for a moment. Then she walked to the window and stood with her back to the room. Belle had never seen her do that before—face away from something instead of toward it.

She stayed that way long enough that Belle stopped waiting for her to turn.

"I built it to protect them," Celeste said finally. Her voice was the same. Everything else was slightly different. "That was the original intention. I want you to know that."

Belle said nothing.

"I know it doesn't change what happened to Angelique." A pause. "I know it doesn't change what happened to you."

She turned then. Her face was composed. But she had waited until it was.

Chapter 85

Celeste poured two glasses of water.

She did not check her phone, which meant she already knew what it would say.

"They'll be back," she said.

Belle shook her head.

"No."

Celeste studied her.

"You're certain."

"Yes."

"Why?"

"Because they don't trust you anymore."

Celeste considered that.

"And they trust you."

Belle sat down for the first time since entering the room.

"They trust that I escaped."

Celeste allowed the smallest trace of a smile.

"No," she said. "They trust that you survived."

Belle said nothing.

Celeste leaned back in her chair.

"The agency still exists," she said.

"Not without them."

"Exactly."

The implication settled slowly between them.

Belle looked up.

"You want me to run it."

Celeste did not deny it.

"They won't work for me," she said. "But they might work for you."

Belle laughed again, but this time the sound held less anger and more disbelief.

"I just spent six weeks caged in an apartment."

"Yes."

"And that makes me qualified to manage women in this business?"

Celeste's eyes sharpened.

"It makes you someone who understands the stakes."

Belle leaned back.

"Why would you give it up?"

Celeste shook her head.

"I'm not giving anything up."

"You just lost everyone."

Celeste gestured toward the room.

"No," she said.

"I lost control."

Another pause.

Then Celeste spoke more quietly.

"I was hired to build this structure. I was never meant to be the face of it."

Belle looked at her carefully.

"You don't own the agency."

Celeste mouth curved slightly.

"No."

Belle looked at her for a moment. All those years of watching Celeste manage rooms, manage men, manage her—and Celeste had been managing someone else's problem the entire time. Not architect. Administrator. The distinction was small and it was everything. She understood then exactly what this conversation was.

"All these years..."

"Yes."

"You were managing someone else's business."

Celeste shrugged.

"I was managing a system."

Belle set down her glass of water. The agency had been the fixed point of her life in New York—the thing that gave the rooms and the hotels and the careful performances their shape. She had believed, without ever examining the belief, that Celeste had built it from something she owned. Something chosen. Now she understood that Celeste had been inside a structure too. A larger one, with walls neither of them had ever seen.

That did not make the offer smaller.

It made it larger in a way Belle had not prepared for.

Belle sat silently for several seconds.

"I need time to think," she said.

Celeste nodded once, as if that too had been anticipated.

Belle picked up her water glass and said nothing further.

She already knew what she was going to do.

What she needed time for was deciding on whose terms she would do it.

Chapter 86

American Airlines flight 3090 touched down at Louis Armstrong at 1:35 pm, fifteen minutes early.

When the doors opened, Belle stood up from 2C, grabbed her overnight bag, and thanked the flight attendant.

At Walgreens on Magazine Street, she bought a disposable phone.

Nothing traceable to a name Celeste owned or a number Pierce had memorized.

She had looked up the number the night before at a library terminal. Written it on the inside of a napkin in ballpoint pen.

The SEC's tip line was staffed. She had expected a recording.

"Securities and Exchange Commission. How can I help you?"

Belle steadied her voice.

"I'd like to report market manipulation. I have specific account information, transaction dates, and the names of the athletes involved."

A pause. The sound of a keyboard.

"Can I get your name?"

"No."

Another pause. Shorter this time.

"Alright. Go ahead."

Belle spoke for four minutes. She did not editorialize. She gave Pierce's full name, his firm, the offshore routing she had memorized from documents she was never supposed to have seen. Dates. Names. The infrastructure of it.

When she finished, the woman on the other end said, "We'll need—"

"That's everything I have," Belle said.

She hung up.

Outside, Magazine Street moved the way New Orleans always moved—without urgency, without apology. Someone was cooking somewhere nearby, something with andouille and thyme.

Belle looked at the napkin.

One number left.

She had written FINRA below the SEC line, because Celeste had once told her that the second call was always the one that mattered. Regulators competed. Competing regulators moved faster.

She had learned that in the townhouse on East Seventy-Sixth Street.

Belle looked at the screen again and began to dial.

Afterward, she walked the three blocks to St. Charles and caught the streetcar to Canal. She turned on Chartres and dropped the phone into a garbage can at Café Fleur de Lis; she ordered brunch. It was mid-afternoon, but this was New Orleans, and the eggs benedict were divine.

Chapter 87

The city knew her by now.

Not by name. New Orleans did not bother with names. It knew her the way it knew everyone who returned a third time—by what they had stopped pretending.

The first time, she had not known what she was walking toward. The second time, grief had sat in her chest like a stone, and New Orleans had given her somewhere to set it down briefly. This time, two crossed-out phone numbers waited on a napkin in her coat pocket, along with a decision she had not yet admitted she had already made.

Southern Decadence had the Quarter again. Rainbow flags on every balcony on Bourbon. Music before noon. The particular quality of light that September produced here—gold and thick, the sun not yet willing to concede the afternoon. Men moved through the streets the way they moved every Labor Day weekend, unhurried, unguarded, the city briefly belonging entirely to people who had decided to stop apologizing for what they wanted.

Two years ago, she had walked these streets for the first time and felt the extraordinary relief of not being watched.

She had been twenty-two and newly formed, and that relief had felt like the most important thing she had ever learned.

Now she walked them and felt something quieter and more permanent. Not relief. Belonging.

Turning off Bourbon onto Toulouse, she let the noise recede behind her, the street narrowing under iron balconies that threw laced shadows across the pavement. By Royal, the Quarter had become itself again—quieter, older, less interested in being seen. A gallery stood open, showing work she couldn't name but recognized now as deliberate, each canvas held in place by the agreement of the room around it. Chicago had taught her that. Without stopping, she crossed Canal, where the street name became St. Charles.

At Poydras she turned toward Mother's.

The lunch rush was in full throat when she arrived. The line moved with the resigned efficiency of people who had decided the wait was worth it, which it was, which was why they were there. She took her place in it without impatience.

The room was everything the Carlyle was not. Linoleum floors worn smooth by decades of people who needed to eat rather than be seen eating. Ceiling fans that worked hard and showed it. The smell of red beans and andouille and coffee that had been keeping since morning. A menu written in chalk above the counter looked like it had not been updated since it was first written.

She ordered the Ferdi special and red beans and rice and took a table near the back.

Around her the room filled and emptied and filled again. A table of contractors in dusty boots. Two women in scrubs splitting a piece of bread pudding. A man eating alone with a paperback propped against his water glass, turning pages without looking up. Tourists identifiable by the slight uncertainty in how they held themselves, as if the city required a posture they hadn't been taught.

Nobody knew her here.

Nobody knew her in New York either, she thought. Not really. They knew Belle Devereaux. They knew what Celeste had built. They knew the woman who walked into the Carlyle without checking her reflection in the elevator.

The question was whether she knew her.

She ate slowly.

She thought about Celeste's offer the way she had learned to think about difficult things—not directly, not all at once, but sideways. Approaching it from the edges and seeing what shape it made.

Celeste had built something real. That was true. The structure worked. The discretion held. The contracts meant something. Women had signed them and been protected by them and left the agency with more than they arrived with.

And Angelique had died inside it.

Celeste had called it a miscalculation. Belle had never found a word for it that felt adequate. Loss was too small. Failure was too clean. What it was, finally, was a cost that the system had absorbed without changing—the way a river absorbed a stone and kept moving, the current closing over the place where it had fallen.

She did not want to run a system that absorbed its losses without changing.

She pushed the plate aside.

But here was the other thing. The thing she had been carrying since she stood in the townhouse and thought *this cannot stay as it is* and meant it.

Once, she had been on the other side of the marble table: young, unformed, and looking for a way out of something small into something larger. To a girl from Mississippi who had never been offered a door before, the contract had meant more than money. *No one touches you without your consent* had not been a sentence. It had been architecture, written by a woman who understood that some things had to be built before they could be believed.

Belle could build that.

And she could mean it in a way Celeste had meant it structurally but not personally.

The question was not whether she was capable.

The question was whether she was willing to carry what it cost.

She sat with that for a while.

The bread pudding arrived that she hadn't ordered. The woman who set it down caught her eye briefly.

"On the house, baby. You look like you thinking too hard."

Belle looked at the bread pudding.

Then she laughed—not the constrained laugh she had learned in the townhouse on Seventy-Sixth Street but a real one, sudden and unguarded, the kind that came from somewhere below the training.

A moth flitted through the room, no light to guide it to its proper destination.

The woman nodded approvingly and moved on.

The bread pudding was delicious.

❧

She walked afterward without direction, letting the Quarter work on her the way it worked on everyone—slowly, through the accumulation of small details that added up to something larger than any of them individually.

On St. Ann she passed a line of party-goers that had materialized from nowhere, a brass band working through something joyful and insistent, a small crowd falling in behind the umbrella with the cheerful inevitability of people who had decided to stop going wherever they were going and go somewhere better instead. The tuba player was enormous, sweating completely through his shirt, playing with his eyes closed.

She watched it pass.

She did not fall in.

She had somewhere to be.

On Conti, she stopped at a small bar she remembered from the second visit—Erin Rose, narrow and dark and cool, a place that had no interest in being discovered because it was already exactly what it intended to be. She ordered a water and sat at the bar, watching the afternoon move past the open door.

The bartender did not ask her anything.

That was the right instinct.

After a while, she paid and walked back toward the river. Not to the tourist stretch by the Moonwalk but further down, past the ferry terminal, where the river was just itself—wide and brown and indifferent, moving toward the Gulf with the unhurried certainty of something that had been doing this long before the city existed and would be doing it long after.

She stood at the railing.

She was not Edna Pontellier. She had settled that the last time she stood near this water. Edna had walked in because she couldn't find a way to own the shore.

Belle already owned it.

The question was what to do with it.

She watched a barge push upstream against the current, slow and deliberate, making progress simply by not stopping.

She turned and walked toward Harrah's.

The casino floor was cold after the heat outside, the air conditioning relentless and democratic, cooling everyone equally regardless of what they had come to lose. Slot machines announced their small victories to the middle distance. A woman at a blackjack table stacked chips with the focused calm of someone who had stopped caring about the outcome and started caring about the execution.

Belle found the roulette table near the back.

She stood and watched two spins without betting.

She was not here because she needed the wheel to decide. She had decided somewhere between the bread pudding she hadn't ordered and the barge pushing upstream against the current. She was here because some decisions deserved a ceremony, however small. A moment of acknowledgment that you were choosing rather than being chosen.

She put a hundred-dollar chip on black.

The croupier's hand moved in its practiced arc. The wheel turned. The ball found its place with the quiet finality of small things that have always known where they were going.

Black.

Of course.

The croupier slid her winnings across the felt.

Belle left them on the table for whoever came next.

She picked up her original chip and walked back out into the New Orleans afternoon.

The heat received her without comment.

A street vendor outside was selling cotton candy.

She took out her phone and booked a flight to New York.

Then she walked back through the Quarter one last time—past the flags and the music and the men moving through the streets without apology, past the antique shop with the chandelier that someone had decided was valuable, past the gallery with the paintings held in place by agreement, past the corner of Dumaine where the small shop sat between two narrow galleries with its door open and its wind chimes turning in the wet air.

She did not go in.

She did not need to.

The moth was already around her neck.

She already knew what it meant.

She walked back to the hotel and packed her bag and did not look back at the city as the cab pulled away, though she felt it watching her go with the particular attention New Orleans reserved for people it expected to see again.

It was not wrong.

❧

Halbrecht called on a Thursday.

Celeste answered on the second ring.

"I understand the situation resolved itself," he said.

"Yes."

A pause.

"My investigators were still working through the building when she walked out," he said. There was no apology in it. Only accuracy.

"I know," Celeste said.

Another pause. Longer.

"An SEC inquiry has begun," Halbrecht said. "Pierce is managing it. He'll manage it badly."

"Yes," Celeste said. "He will."

Halbrecht was quiet for a moment.

"She's quite something," he said. Not warmly. The way you note a fact that has earned acknowledgment.

Celeste looked at the folder on her desk with Pierce's name on it.

"Yes," she said. "She is."

The call ended.

Celeste set the phone down.

Neither of them had said her name.

Chapter 88

"They'll only come back if things change."

Celeste nodded once.

"That's why you're here."

Belle looked around the room. The table. The folders. The quiet machinery of Celeste's operation.

Two months ago, Pierce had tried to take control of her life.

Now Celeste was offering something far more strange.

Power.

Belle exhaled slowly.

"Then we rebuild it differently."

Celeste lifted her glass.

"Good," she said.

Chapter 89

The doorbell rang at eight-thirty.

Belle had not slept. She had sat at the kitchen table since the conversation with Celeste ended, her coffee going cold in stages, the two of them occupying the apartment's silence the way people occupy a waiting room—present, separately, not yet ready to leave.

When the bell rang Celeste stood without being asked.

"I'll give you the room," she said.

She moved down the hallway without hesitation, past Angelique's closed door—not pausing, not looking at it, the way you didn't look at certain things because looking changed nothing and cost everything—and into Belle's bedroom. The door closed quietly behind her.

Belle opened the front door.

Leila stood on the stoop.

Behind her, Mei and two others Belle recognized, coats pulled tight against the morning cold, their expressions carrying the particular resolution of women who had decided something and come to say it in person rather than by phone.

Leila looked at her the way she had always looked at her. Not with warmth. With assessment. Taking inventory of what six weeks had done and what it hadn't.

"You're thinner," she said.

"I'm fine," Belle said.

"I know you're fine." Leila's voice carried the same quality it always had—quiet, precise, the kind that didn't need volume to land. "I said you're thinner."

Belle stepped aside.

They came in carefully, the way people entered apartments where something had broken and not yet been repaired. One of them glanced down the hallway. Angelique's door. Still closed. The glass Belle had left upside down on the bathroom counter still there, exactly where Angelique had placed it the last morning she left.

Nobody said anything about it.

They sat at the kitchen table. Belle put the kettle on.

“How did you get out?” Leila said.

Not quite a question. The thing she had come to establish first—not out of curiosity but out of the practical necessity of a woman who needed to know whether the person across from her was capable before she said anything further.

“He took me downstairs,” Belle said.

Leila waited.

“He thought I was ready to go with him. By then, my notes were already in other hands. In the lobby, I told him they would become public if he touched me or my mother.” She set the tea down without ceremony. “Then I walked away.”

The two women behind Leila exchanged a look.

Leila did not look away from Belle.

“Calculated,” she said.

“It had to be.”

Leila nodded once. The nod of someone filing something away in a place they intended to return to.

"Celeste knew," Mei said.

"She suspected," Belle said.

"Same thing."

Belle sat down.

"She didn't call the police because the police would have examined everything. Every client. Every contract. Every woman in this building." She wrapped both hands around her cup. "She wasn't wrong about the math."

"She was wrong about Angelique," Leila said quietly.

The name landed the way it always did now. With weight. With the particular gravity of something that could not be undone and had stopped needing to be discussed to be present.

Belle looked at the table.

"Yes," she said. "She was."

The silence that followed was not uncomfortable. It was the silence of people who had already grieved and were now on the other side of it, in the territory where grief becomes something you carry rather than something that carries you.

After a moment one of the women spoke.

"We're not going back to her."

"I know," Belle said.

The woman looked at Leila.

Leila looked at Belle.

"You escaped him," she said. "You reported him. You came back." A pause. "Nobody told you to do any of those things."

"No."

"Celeste would have calculated the exposure. Weighed the risk. Found the most efficient solution." Leila leaned forward slightly—the same small gesture Belle remembered from years ago at the dining table in the townhouse, when she had told Belle to stop performing and start being deliberate. "You just did it. Because it was right and because you were angry and because you understood exactly what he was."

She held Belle's gaze.

"That's not training," she said. "That's character."

Belle felt the words land somewhere specific and permanent.

She had not expected that from Leila.

She was not certain she deserved it.

Belle's bedroom door opened.

Celeste came back down the hallway. She moved past Angelique's door the same way she had before—without pausing, without looking—and entered the kitchen.

She took in the room in one pass. The women. The tea. Belle at the table.

Something crossed her face that was not quite surprise. The expression of a woman watching a calculation resolve exactly as she had modeled it, slightly ahead of schedule.

"So," she said.

Leila did not stand.

"We're done," she said. "With the current arrangement."

Celeste moved to the counter and poured herself a glass of water. Her hands were steady. They were always steady.

"I expected that."

"We thought you might."

Celeste turned.

"And?"

Leila glanced at Belle.

"We'll work for her."

Celeste looked at Belle then. Not surprised. Something more complicated than satisfied—the expression of a woman who had built something carefully over many years and was now watching it become something she had not entirely planned and could not entirely control, deciding in real time whether that was failure or completion.

Belle felt the weight of every eye in the room.

"I haven't agreed to anything," she said.

Leila's mouth moved. Not quite a smile.

"You came back," she said. "You could have gone anywhere. You came back to this address." She set her cup down. "That's agreement."

Belle looked at the table.

The kitchen was quiet. Angelique's kitchen. The cabinet she had always closed too hard. The chair she had always pulled too far from the table and never pushed back in. The particular smell of the apartment that was still partly hers even now—something floral underneath the coffee, faint enough that Belle sometimes thought she had imagined it and then caught it again.

She thought about what it meant to sit at this table and make rules.

She thought about the women who would sit across from her the way she had once sat across from Celeste—young and unformed and looking for a door. She thought about what she owed them. Efficiency would not be enough. Neither would another system that absorbed its losses without changing.

It had to be something real.

She looked up.

"If we rebuild this," she said, "it's not the same rules."

No one objected.

She looked at Leila.

"No more clients like Pierce. Anyone who tests a boundary loses access. No revenue exceptions."

Leila nodded.

"No silence if someone disappears. Anyone. Police, lawyers, whatever it takes. The business absorbs the exposure."

One of the other women exhaled slowly.

"Agreed."

Belle looked at the closed door at the end of the hallway.

She held it for a moment.

"And Angelique doesn't get filed under miscalculation." Her voice stayed even. "She gets acknowledged. By name. As someone this system failed. That gets said out loud before we do anything else. We tell her family the truth."

The room was very quiet.

Even Celeste nodded.

Belle looked at her.

Two women across a kitchen table in an apartment on Seventy-Fifth Street. One of them had built something. One of them was about to change it. Between them the particular silence of a transaction that had no paperwork and required none.

"You can stay," Belle said. "If you want."

Celeste tilted her head.

"Stay?"

"Your contacts. Your knowledge. Your judgment on configurations." Belle held her gaze. "But not your rules."

Something moved across Celeste's face. Brief. The expression of a woman setting something down she had been carrying for a long time, and was only now admitting, had been heavy.

"You realize," she said quietly, "that I built this for exactly this."

Belle waited.

"Not for myself," Celeste said. "For whoever came after me and understood it well enough to change it."

The admission sat in the room.

Belle believed it.

She also believed Celeste had not known it was true until this moment.

"Then stay," Belle said.

Celeste looked at her for a long moment.

Then she smiled. Not the composed smile she used in rooms where she needed something. The other one. The one Belle had seen perhaps twice before and had never been able to fully read.

"Belle," she said.

"Yes."

"You've already taken the job."

The room relaxed then, the tension releasing the way it released after a long silence finally broken—not dramatically, just incrementally, each person settling back into themselves.

One of the women laughed softly.

"Well," she said.

"I suppose we have a madame."

Belle shook her head.

"No, a manager," she said.

"Just someone making sure the system remembers who it's supposed to protect."

Outside the apartment windows, New York moved through another ordinary morning—taxis and delivery trucks and men in dark coats walking with phones pressed to their ears, the city indifferent as always to the private revolutions occurring in the rooms above it.

Inside, the agency began again.

Chapter 90

The men arrived at seven-fifteen.

They did not come through the trading floor or the public entrance on Park Avenue, where the firm's name was etched in limestone above the door.

They came to Pierce's apartment.

Four of them. Dark coats. Credentials presented without theater, the way professionals presented credentials when they already knew the door would open because the alternative was worse.

Pierce answered in a gray cashmere robe.

He looked at the credentials.

He looked at the four men.

His face did not change.

"I'll need to call my attorney," he said.

"Of course," the lead agent said pleasantly.

They waited in the foyer while he made the call. One of them stood near the window. One near the door. The other two simply stood, the way men stand when they have already accounted for every variable in the room and found none of them interesting.

Pierce's attorney arrived forty minutes later.

By then, a second team had entered the firm's offices on Park Avenue.

The conference room overlooking the avenue—the one Halbrecht had used for private meetings, the one with no assistants and a single folder on the table—was sealed at eight-oh-two.

Halbrecht was already at his desk when his assistant appeared in the doorway.

"There are federal agents in the building," she said.

Halbrecht looked up from the document he was reading.

He set it down.

He had known, in the abstract, that this moment existed somewhere in the future. He had done the math on it repeatedly over the past year—the exposure, the liability, the precise point at which Pierce's private arrangements would cease to be Pierce's private problem and become the firm's.

He had not known the math would resolve this quickly.

He had also not known—and this was the part he found himself returning to, sitting very still at his desk while the city moved below the window with its usual indifference—that someone had made two phone calls from a disposable phone.

Not Celeste.

He had underestimated the woman in the photographs.

He had looked at her posture in the lobby security stills and thought *controlled*.

He should have thought *patient*.

There was a difference.

He straightened the document on his desk.

Then he picked up his phone and called his own attorney.

Chapter 91

The woman arrived on time.

Precisely when the appointment said.

Belle noticed that.

She noticed the way the woman paused in the doorway before entering—not hesitating, just allowing the room a moment to register her. She noticed the coat, which was good but not aggressive. The shoes, which were practical with a quiet heel. The way she held her bag—not clutched, not dangling, simply carried.

She noticed that the woman's eyes went to the window before they went to Belle.

That was either nerves or intelligence.

Belle waited to find out which.

"Sit down," she said.

The woman sat. Her posture was careful without being rigid. She folded her hands in her lap and looked across the table with the expression of someone who had prepared for this and was now trying to decide whether the preparation had been adequate.

Belle let the silence sit for a moment.

The woman did not fill it.

That was the answer.

"Tell me something about yourself that isn't on the page Celeste sent me," Belle said.

The woman considered that carefully.

"I grew up in a place where being smart wasn't an asset," she said finally. "I learned early to make it look like something else."

Belle studied her.

"What did you make it look like?"

"Charm," the woman said. "Until I understood that charm wasn't really that valuable."

Belle felt something shift in the room. Bpth of them relaxed their shoulders the tiniest amount.

Not recognition exactly. Something more specific than that.

She leaned forward slightly.

"What's your name?" she asked. Not because she didn't know. Because she wanted to hear how the woman said it.

"Dani," she said.

Then, after a beat—the right length of beat:

"For now."

Belle looked at her for a long moment.

Outside on Seventy-Sixth Street, the city moved through another afternoon—taxis and delivery trucks and women walking with the particular purpose of people who had somewhere to be and had decided to get there on their own terms.

Inside, the table held its silence.

Belle picked up the pen.

"Tell me what you know about consequence," she said.

And she began to listen.

Chapter 92

The call was scheduled for ten.

By nine fifty-eight, thirty-two small rectangles filled Belle's screen. Women in robes and women in blazers. Women with coffee. Women in what looked like parking lots and hotel lobbies, and one who was clearly still in bed with her camera angled carefully at the ceiling. A woman in New Orleans sitting on what Belle recognized as a wrought iron balcony, the Quarter visible behind her in the early morning light. Three women in a shared frame in Chicago, crowded together on a couch like they had decided there was safety in proximity. Las Vegas arriving last, two women, one of them eating something she didn't bother to hide.

Celeste's rectangle was in the upper left corner. Composed. Still. A background so neutral it could have been painted.

At ten o'clock exactly, Celeste spoke.

"Thank you all for being here." Her voice carried the same quality it always carried—calm, precise, the voice of a woman who had never needed volume to be heard. "I want to introduce someone. Most of you know my name. Very few of you know her yet. That's going to change."

She paused.

"Belle Devereaux."

Celeste's rectangle went quiet. She didn't step away from the camera. She simply settled back slightly, the way a person settles when they have finished one thing and are waiting for the next to begin. The reins passed in a single sentence without anyone having to name them.

Belle looked at the screen. Thirty-two women looking back at her. Some curious. Some cautious. The woman in Las Vegas had stopped eating.

"I started in the business the way we all did," Belle said.

She let that sit for a moment.

"Someone saw something in me I hadn't figured out how to see in myself yet. Offered me a door. I walked through it because the alternative was staying somewhere that was going to cost me more than I was willing to pay."

A few of the rectangles shifted. Small movements. Women adjusting in their chairs, their expressions changing in ways that weren't quite recognition but were close to it.

"I've been in New York for a few years now. I know some of you by name. Most of you I don't know yet. That matters to me—that I don't know you yet. I want to fix that."

She looked at the camera directly.

"But before I tell you what's changing and why, I need to tell you about someone."

The screen went very still.

"Her name was Angelique. She worked in New York. She was extraordinary at this work—composed, precise, the kind of woman who could read a room before she'd fully entered it." Belle paused. "She was my roommate. She was the first person in this city who told me the truth about how to survive it."

She did not look away from the camera.

"She died inside this system. Not because she was careless. Because the system she was operating in had margins it hadn't told her about. Margins it expected her to absorb."

A woman in Chicago had her hand over her mouth. The woman on the New Orleans balcony was very still.

"I'm telling you her name because she deserves to be named. And because the reason I'm sitting here instead of someone else is that I watched what happened to her, and I decided I wasn't willing to run something that filed its losses under miscalculation and moved on."

"There will be a fund in her name. For women new to the city who don't have someone like her in the next room."

She let the silence sit the way she had learned to let silence sit.

"So. Here's what's changing."

❧

She spoke for twenty minutes.

No slides. No prepared remarks. Just the things she had decided in a kitchen in New Orleans eating bread pudding she hadn't ordered, standing at the railing watching a barge push upstream, sitting across from Celeste with four women who had come to the apartment because they'd decided trust had to be rebuilt from something real.

No clients who tested boundaries. Anyone who pushed lost access. No revenue exceptions, no matter who the client was or what he represented.

No silence if something went wrong. Police, lawyers, whatever it took. The business absorbed the exposure. That was the cost of doing this correctly, and she was prepared to pay it.

Screening tightened. Not just financial verification. Behavioral history. References checked through channels Celeste hadn't used before. It would slow things down. That was acceptable.

Every woman on the call had a direct line to Belle. Not an assistant. Not a coordinator. Her.

"If something feels wrong," Belle said, "you leave. You don't calculate the fee. You don't finish the evening. You go. And you call me."

She looked at the screen.

"Those are the rules. They're not negotiable, and they don't have exceptions. If you have questions about how they apply to a specific situation, ask me. That's what the direct line is for."

A woman in Los Angeles spoke first. Her camera was good, her background deliberately neutral, her expression carrying the particular careful attention of someone who had been doing this long enough to know what questions mattered.

"What happens if a client complains? If he says we were difficult, unprofessional?"

"I handle it," Belle said.

"How?"

"However it needs to be handled." Belle held her gaze through the screen. "He loses access. If he makes noise, we make more. Men in his position don't want noise."

The Los Angeles woman considered that.

"And if Celeste disagrees with how you handle it?"

Celeste's rectangle didn't move.

Belle almost smiled.

"Celeste recruits," she said. "I manage. We've divided the work cleanly." She paused. "You can ask her yourself."

Every rectangle shifted toward Celeste's corner of the screen.

Celeste looked at the camera with the expression Belle had seen twice before and never been able to fully read.

"Belle is correct," Celeste said simply.

The Los Angeles woman nodded once. Slowly. The nod of someone filing something away in a place they intended to return to.

A woman in Chicago—one of the three on the couch—leaned forward.

"Angelique," she said. "Did her family know? What actually happened?"

Belle looked at her directly.

"Not yet," she said. "That's the next thing I'm doing."

The Chicago woman sat back.

The woman in New Orleans on the balcony spoke for the first time. Her voice was low and unhurried, carrying the particular cadence of someone the city had shaped over time.

"You said you started the way we all did," she said. "Someone saw something in you."

"Yes."

"Who was that?"

Belle looked at Celeste's rectangle in the upper left corner of the screen.

"The same person who found most of you," she said.

Celeste's expression didn't change.

But something behind it did.

❧

The call ended at eleven twenty-three.

The rectangles disappeared one by one until the screen held only Belle's reflection in the black.

She sat with it for a moment.

Thirty-two women who had listened. Some convinced. Some still deciding. The woman in Las Vegas who had stopped eating and never started again. The three on the couch in Chicago who had leaned incrementally closer as the call went on, until by the end they were nearly touching.

Celeste's rectangle had been the last to go.

She had not said goodbye.

She had simply looked at Belle for one long moment before the screen went dark.

Belle understood it the way she understood most things Celeste communicated without words.

You'll do.

She closed the laptop.

Outside on Seventy-Sixth Street the city moved through another ordinary morning, indifferent as always to the private revolutions occurring in the rooms above it.

Belle reopened the laptop.

She had a letter to write.

Chapter 93

Dear Mr. and Mrs. Meeks,

My name is Belle Devereaux. I worked with your daughter in New York. I have been trying to write this letter for longer than I want to admit, and I apologize for the time it has taken. Some things resist being put into words, and Angelique deserves words that are right rather than words that are simply prompt.

I want to tell you about her, if you'll allow me.

I met Angelique when I first came to New York. I didn't know anyone. I didn't know the city. I was twenty-two, and I believed I was more prepared than I was, which is a particular kind of young that New York corrects quickly and without sentiment. Angelique was my roommate. She was already here, already settled, already the kind of woman the city had shaped into something precise and sure of itself. I was none of those things yet.

She didn't make a project of me. That was the first thing I noticed. She didn't offer unsolicited advice or take it upon herself to explain how things worked. She simply lived alongside me with a patience and a steadiness that I have come to understand, only in her absence, was a form of generosity I didn't have the vocabulary for at the time.

One evening, she appeared in the kitchen doorway holding a bottle of wine that cost less than the glasses we usually used and said, "I hate drinking alone," as if that settled it. We sat at the kitchen table for two hours. We talked about small things. Ordinary things. A restaurant she liked on Lexington. A coat she'd seen in a window on Madison that she couldn't justify and couldn't stop thinking about. It was the first evening since arriving in New York that I forgot to be careful.

She had a way of telling you important things as if they were obvious. Not lecturing. Simply passing along what she knew the way you hand someone an umbrella when you can see it's going to rain. She did it without ceremony and without requiring gratitude and I have thought about it almost every day since she died.

She was loved here. I want you to know that clearly and without qualification. By the women she worked with, who are scattered across this city and others, and who speak her name with the particular care people reserve for those who mattered to them in ways that are difficult to explain. She built things in people without meaning to. She left them steadier than she found them.

The hospitality industry is not always kind to the people inside it. It asks for composure in circumstances that don't deserve it. It rewards the appearance of ease over the reality of effort. Angelique had both—the composure and the effort beneath it—and she wore them without complaint and without asking to be acknowledged for it. She was, in the truest sense of the word, a professional. The people she worked alongside were better at their work for having known her.

I have established a small fund in her name. It will support women new to New York who are navigating the industry without the benefit of someone like her in the next room. I hope that is alright with you. It felt like the right shape for what she left behind.

I am sorry for your loss. I am sorry it took me this long to write. I am sorry that the version of her life you knew was necessarily incomplete—that is not a criticism of her or of you, only an acknowledgment that she was a private person who kept her worlds carefully separate, which is its own kind of dignity.

What I can tell you, without reservation, is that the world she built here was real. The women in it were real. The care she took with them was real.

Angelique was extraordinary in the rarest way: she knew it without needing to be told.

With sincerity and with gratitude for the woman you raised,

Belle Devereaux

She folded the letter, placed it into an envelope, and began to write the address.

Epilogue—The Cotton Boll Queen

The cotton was open when she drove in.

White across the fields like something that had already happened.

Yazoo City had not changed. It had only tightened.

Eudora Watson stood outside the church in her good black coat, watching Belle's car turn into the lot the way a woman watches for something she has been expecting. She was thicker through the middle than Belle remembered, her hair gone fully silver, but she stood with the same particular stillness that had once made Betsy say, that woman could out-wait a stone.

They held each other without speaking first.

Eudora smelled like gardenia and coffee and something Belle associated specifically with the house outside Yazoo City, with Sunday mornings and the ceiling fan turning slow overhead.

"Her body just couldn't outlast it," Eudora said finally, her voice low and even, her chin lifting slightly the way she spoke when she wanted something understood rather than argued with. "All them years before. They had to have their say eventually."

Belle nodded.

"She fought it," Eudora added. "Right up until she didn't."

"I know she did."

Eudora pulled back and looked at her with the direct unhurried attention she had always given to things that mattered.

"Them last years were good ones," she said. "She knew that. She told me so, more than once."

Belle looked toward the church door, toward the cotton fields beyond the parking lot, white and still in the morning light.

"Thank you," she said. "For all of it."

Eudora made a small sound that dismissed gratitude without dismissing the feeling behind it.

"She was worth it," she said. "Every bit."

They walked inside together.

☙

Inside the church fellowship hall, aluminum trays sweated on folding tables. Women who had known Betsy in every version of herself stood in careful clusters.

Belle felt the stare before she saw its source.

“Annabelle Crump,” the woman said, drawing the old name out like a thread.

Tanya Rawlins.

Homecoming court, senior year. Blonde then. Still blonde now but assisted.

Tanya had once said it in the hallway outside second-period English, loud enough for others to hear: *Look at her, thinks she's some Cotton Boll Queen.*

It had meant white trash playing royalty. Dirt pretending to be crown.

Now Tanya looked at her differently.

“You clean up well,” Tanya added.

Belle let the silence sit.

“I’ve always been clean,” she said evenly.

A flicker crossed Tanya’s face—memory catching up with the present.

"Caleb Rush died," Tanya said, "Few years back. You heard?"

"No," Belle said.

Tanya nodded, as if that settled something.

Someone behind them whispered, “That’s her? The one in New York?”

Tanya’s eyes returned to Belle’s dress, the watch, the posture that did not bend.

“You always did think you were better than this place,” Tanya said.

“No,” Belle replied. “I thought I could leave it.”

That landed.

Tanya glanced toward the cemetery windows, toward the fields beyond.

“Well,” she said finally, almost laughing, but not quite. “I guess you are the Cotton Boll Queen after all.”

This time there was no derision in it.

Only acknowledgment.

A coronation issued reluctantly.

Belle did not smile.

“Queens,” she said calmly, “don’t campaign.”

She stepped past her.

The phrase moved through the room differently now. Not a joke. Not a jab. A story people could tell about her that did not require understanding her.

❧

Outside, the morning had gone very still.

The kind of still that happened sometimes in August in Mississippi—not peaceful, just suspended, as if the heat had decided to hold its breath. The cotton in the fields beyond the cemetery fence stood without moving. White and open and waiting the way it always waited, the way it had waited her entire childhood, patient as something that knew it would outlast everything planted near it.

Belle stood at the grave alone for a moment before the others came out.

The marker was simple. Betsy had specified that—or rather Belle had specified it on Betsy's behalf, because Betsy in her last months had been specific about small things in the way people sometimes became specific when they understood that small things were what remained. No scripture. No dates except the ones that mattered. Just the name.

Elizabeth Anne Crump.

No Davidson. No Johnson. None of the men who had accumulated in her life over all the years.

Just Crump. The name she had given her daughter.

Belle looked at it for a long time.

The pendant lay against her collarbone, warm in the August heat. She pressed two fingers to it without meaning to—the same gesture Angelique had made once, pressing two fingers to her sternum, the signal that meant *you go, you don't calculate, you just g o*—and felt the metal solid and certain beneath her hand.

The cotton shifted.

Not from wind—there was no wind. Just a single movement, one row of bolls turning slightly on their stems the way cotton sometimes turned in the absolute stillness of an August morning, as if the field were adjusting its position. As if it were settling.

Belle watched it happen.

She thought of the night Caleb had gone down into the rows. Of the wind that had dropped and then returned. Of the land that had raised her and not intended to surrender her easily and had, in the end, let her go.

She was back now.

Not to stay.

Just to stand here for a moment and let the land see what she had become.

The cotton stilled again.

Belle lowered her hand from the pendant.

She had been gone a long time. She had become someone the fields would not recognize. Someone Betsy had not entirely known and had loved anyway, in the particular way Betsy loved things—imperfectly, intermittently, genuinely.

You go see her. You don't owe this place nothin.

She had gone.

She had seen.

She had come back to say so.

Thank you, she thought. Not to Betsy or the cotton fields, exactly. To something that didn't have a name and didn't need one.

Then the church door opened behind her, and people began to come out. Billy moved apart from the group the way men like Billy always moved apart, and the moment was over.

❧

After the graveside service, Billy stood with Belle.

Thinner. Smaller. The right hand still not closing fully. Two fingers bent inward permanently.

When he approached, he kept that hand half-hidden.

"Annabelle," he said.

She looked at him.

He flexed the fingers unconsciously.

"They don't set right in there," he said. "You don't always get proper care."

"In where?" she asked.

He met her eyes.

"Prison."

She tilted her head slightly.

"You committed a felony," she said. "Men do unpredictable things when they're confined."

It was not an answer.

It was not a denial.

He swallowed.

"I ain't touched another woman," he said.

"That seems prudent."

Behind them, Tanya Rawlins watched.

So did half the town.

They would decide what had happened long before any truth surfaced.

Belle did not need to control the narrative.

She only needed to occupy it.

At the reception, she wrote a check to the church—large enough to matter, small enough to avoid spectacle. The church secretary looked at the signature—AB Devereaux—without comment.

She announced a scholarship in Betsy's name for literature students at Yazoo City High.

"Edgar Allan Poe," she said quietly when asked why.

Edgar Allan Poe.

Her mother had loved tragedy.

Belle preferred architecture.

She got into the car, *The Awakening* on the seat beside her, and drove away.

In the rearview mirror the cotton remained perfectly still.

Queens do not wave to territory, she thought.

They own it quietly.

"but whatever came, she had resolved never again to belong to another than herself." —— Kate Chopin, The Awakening

For fans of Belle Devereaux

Two bonus chapters are available exclusively to readers of The Cotton Boll Queen.

Chicago, Night One—the evening Celeste sent Annabelle to the city alone, before New York.

What Eudora Knew—fifteen years in the house on County Road 7.

To receive them, visit ltpublishing.com/belle or scan below.

www.ingramcontent.com/pod-product-compliance
Lightning Source LLC
LaVergne TN
LVHW091249110826
845146LV00002BA/582